Artist Free Zone

Annette Mori

ALSO BY ANNETTE MORI

ARTIST FREE ZONE

ANNETTE MORI

Affinity
Rainbow Publications

2022

Artist Free Zone
© 2019 by Annette Mori

Affinity E-Book Press NZ LTD.
Canterbury, New Zealand

Edition - Reprint 2022

ISBN: 978-1-99-004988-0 (paperback)
ISBN: 978-1-99-004985-9 (EPUB)
ISBN: 978-1-99-004986-6 (PDF)
ISBN: 978-1-99-004987-3 (KINDLE)

Editor: Rogena Mitchell-Jones
Cover Design: Irish Dragon Designs
Production Design: Affinity Publication Services

ACKNOWLEDGMENTS

A huge thank you to all of my beta readers: Gail Dodge, Carrie Camp, Ameliah Faith, Cathie Williamson, Darla Baker, Dana Holmes, and Elle Hyden, who made great suggestions to improve the initial draft. I would also like to express my gratitude to Affinity Rainbow Publications and the wonderful trio—JM Dragon, Erin O'Reilly, and Nancy Kaufman—who agreed to republish this work. I am eternally grateful for the opportunities they give me to let my stories see the light of day. My family members who are also very supportive, include my nephew, Aaron and his wife, Chelsea, and my older sister. Thanks to Rogena Mitchell-Jones for her magic as the final editor to tighten the story. Thanks to Nancy Kaufman for the final cover. A huge thank you to all the other readers and fellow writers who have sent personal e-mails, written reviews and posted nice things on Facebook (you know who you are). Finally, my wife, Jody, continues her support even when it interferes with our time.

DEDICATION

To my beautiful wife who showed me that a person can find "the one" later in life. It is never too late to achieve that happily ever after. And, to my beloved kitties Gizmo and Chewy who I know are watching over me from kitty heaven.

TABLE OF CONTENTS

PROLOGUE

Sarasota

Sarasota lifted her azure eyes to the weeping woman. Her brother curled into the woman's left side as she absently ran her fingers through his soft baby fine hair.

Her human companion was crying softly for the third day in a row as she lifted Sarasota into her arms. Sarasota didn't mind getting wet, even though she would normally avoid water. Her human needed her. It was the responsibility of her and her brother to cheer Melissa up.

Melissa grabbed a tissue from the box on the nightstand and blew, waking up Freud, who expressed his displeasure with a stunted, "Meow."

"Sorry, Freud. I know I'm a mess. Something is wrong with me. I keep doing the same thing over and over, and every single one of them leaves. Am I such a horrible lover I'm destined for a life of loneliness? What do I keep doing wrong to drive them all away? I'm so tempted to have a doctor prescribe a happy pill for me. I know it's situational depression, but maybe I can convince them it's full-blown clinical depression."

Sarasota didn't want to see Melissa in so much pain, but what could she do? After all, she was only a cat.

CHAPTER ONE

Melissa

"Um, babe."

"Yeah," I answered without looking up from my book. I wasn't paying attention. I did that a lot—you know, answer without my partner seeing the whites of my eyes. It meant I wasn't listening. No eye contact was a bad habit. I admit it. It was a treat to have Colette visit on a Monday night, and I wasn't spending quality time with her. It wasn't right. I knew that.

"We need to talk," Colette said.

Oh shit. I decided I'd better listen because those are the scariest four words in the English language. In my experience, no good ever came from those four words. When your lover says them, it doesn't mean they want to talk. It means they have something bad to tell you. That wasn't a conversation.

I looked up from my book and showed her the whites of my eyes. I knew I needed to demonstrate I was listening.

Colette continued, "I know it's not a surprise that things haven't been working between us lately."

Well, call me stupid because it *was* a surprise. Yeah, we had a few problems a year earlier when I found out Colette was drinking again. I defended her to all my friends who kept telling me she wasn't only off the wagon but had tipped the damn thing completely over. We had been to counseling and were on a good path I thought. We even had ourselves a fabulous mini vacation. Two weeks ago, I braved that itty-bitty scary-ass float plane and gave her the best fortieth birthday present—a trip to Stehekin, Washington. You can only get there by boat or float plane, and she always wanted to go by plane. One of my biggest fears was flying, yet I endured that airborne coffin for her. Why? Because it's what you do when you love someone. I loved her more than my phobia.

"What do you mean? I thought we were doing okay. Didn't you love our time in Stehekin?" I looked at her with hope in my eyes.

"Well, yes, we had a nice time in Stehekin, and that was sweet of you to take me there, but you've got to admit, even on vacation, we aren't exactly tearing up the sheets. I just don't think it's going to work out. I need more in a relationship, and I'm not getting that from you."

Are you fucking kidding me? Normally, the f-word wasn't in my vocabulary unless I had an especially good reason, but that didn't mean I didn't think it.

I wondered if she'd met someone else but couldn't imagine she'd had time to have an affair.

That didn't stop me from asking because artist number one and artist number two—my previous two long-term relationships—both left me for someone else.

"Did you meet someone?"

She looked up at me, and her eyes grew wide. "No. That's not what this is about. It's about how you sequester yourself in the office the minute you get home. We've been drifting apart for years."

I became defensive and spit out, "I *sequester* myself in the office because I'm constantly working on your website to help you sell your music, sign you up for your college classes, and help you with your homework."

Okay, maybe my beeline into the office each night wasn't a completely selfless gesture. I'm a huge introvert, and my job as a human resource director needed me to be front and center with people all day. By the time I got home, all I wanted to do was hide away in the office until my juices regenerated. Working on her website and helping her with other computer projects gave me the perfect excuse not to have a deep conversation about anything.

I thought I detected a note of apology in her voice as she answered, "I know, and I appreciate all you've done for me. Really, I do. It's just we never talk. I don't ever know what you're thinking about. You keep yourself all bottled up. I can't be with someone like that."

"I know. I'm sorry. It's just such a habit. I forget I only get to see you on weekends and I should spend all my time with you—not on the computer. The PowerPoint you needed to do for your class was important. I tried to work on it when you were asleep this past weekend. I guess I got too involved and forgot the time. I'll try harder to talk more."

Colette had been attending school in Seattle for the past year and a half, and not every subject came easily to her. Her classwork took every ounce of extra time during the week for her to complete. She had a place in Seattle she stayed at Monday through Friday, but she almost always came to our house in Cle Elum on the weekends.

Of course, I was paying for her schooling and for most of her living expenses since we got together eight years ago.

We had a plan for our future. Colette had almost finished with respiratory school, and then we could pay off our bills and retire early.

Colette was artist number three. I could sure pick 'em. I mostly supported all my previous long-term girlfriends who were artists. Like a bee to honey, I could never resist the starving artist types. They were all incredibly talented but not terribly motivated to hold down a full-time job.

"I don't want to hurt you, but I don't think you can change enough to meet my needs," Colette said.

"But we have eight years together. I'll do anything. I'll go to counseling again. Whatever you want, but please don't leave." At this point, I wasn't above begging.

"I'm sorry. I have to go."

Well, fuck me raw. Again, I didn't say this aloud. I only thought it.

Instead, I asked, "Are you leaving me?"

She wasn't completely heartless, I suppose, as she began to cry a little. That didn't stop her from asking for a favor. "Do you think you can take care of Red and Blackie until I can work out arrangements for them at my place?"

"Sure. Okay." Even though I'm a cat person and Red and Blackie were her dogs, I agreed. Taking care of her dogs was one of the ways I showed her my love. I even had a fence built at the new place I bought in Cle Elum, just for her dogs.

I moved to Cle Elum for a new job as the human resources director because the politics at my old hospital led me to believe my days might be numbered. In a very controversial election, I supported the losing candidate for a position on the hospital board. The surgeon who won was a crazy son of a bitch who was vindictive enough to get me fired. When the community elected him, I might have used the term 'crazy mother fucker' with my close friends because that was one of those times when using the f-word was totally justified.

Colette stood at the door and hugged me goodbye. "Take care of yourself, Melissa. I'll call you later to get my stuff."

"Okay," I responded. What else could I say? I was still in shock. The tears hadn't started yet.

I closed the door on artist number three.

Sitting on the loveseat, I looked out the window. I'd bought a house in a quiet little cookie cutter neighborhood. Every other home on the block looked the same except for mine.

When the realtor showed us the little house that resembled a ski chalet, I fell in love with it. I told Colette to take off her shoes the minute I stepped into the house because this was it—the place I would buy. I didn't want the carpets messed up with our snow-encrusted shoes.

Now I thought how pitiful I was in my unique little house, and how this was the perfect fit for my lonely existence.

CHAPTER TWO

Colette

Everyone thinks it's easy to be the one who ends a long-term relationship, but it's not. When I looked into Melissa's soft brown eyes, I knew I was breaking her heart. I knew I would be the one blamed for the demise of our love. It didn't matter that we'd been living as roommates for the last two years. All the passion had slowly leaked out like the air in one of those cheap air mattresses. I'd been down this road before. I even wrote a song about it called "My Foul Mood" when I ended my last long-term relationship way before I met Melissa.

I was certain I'd finally met my soulmate. How could I help Melissa understand this? I told her the lie because I still cared deeply for her, and I knew if I told the truth, I'd hurt her even more, maybe destroy her.

"Is there someone else?"

"No, of course not," I had lied.

"Then, I don't understand why we can't at least try to work this out," she pleaded.

What could I say? I couldn't tell her that over the Fourth of July weekend when I was working at Hollybrook, I'd met the most amazing woman, and for me, this was a game changer.

"It's too late for that. We've already been through counseling, and it hasn't worked. I think it's time we realized it's not going to work out between us."

I knew I was asking a lot when I wanted her to take care of Red and Blackie, but they were both innocents in this mess. They didn't have anywhere to go. I was in a bind. Melissa wasn't even a dog person, but that's the kind of woman she was—if you asked, she'd oblige. She agreed to take care of them until I could make other arrangements. I felt like a total shit, but what else could I do?

I told her to take care of herself. I knew how lame that sounded. I wanted to tell her I still loved her, but I couldn't stay in a relationship that was literally choking the life out of me. Although I had her undying support, she kept a major part of herself at arm's length. I wondered if she would ever let anyone close to her. There was a big part of Melissa no one touched, and I needed all of her, not what she thought was enough to keep us together.

I suspected her first love broke her heart beyond repair. All I'd done was smash the remaining pieces into smaller bits. She was broken well before I came into the picture. She'd never admit it, but I knew all along I couldn't touch the part of her I longed to reach. If it hadn't happened in eight years, it would never happen.

She stood at the door to her chalet and watched me walk out of her life. I saw her blink a few times, but the tears never came. I wasn't surprised. Melissa never cried. Maybe it wasn't so bad. Maybe I hadn't broken her heart after all.

†

Climbing into my truck, I reached for my phone. I told Serena I would call her as soon as I had the talk with Melissa. I'd driven a few miles down the road before I pulled to the side and then punched in her number.

"Hey," I said.

"How'd it go?"

"Okay, I guess."

"Did you tell her about us?"

"No, I lied. It's not something I'm proud of right now." My tears fell.

"Oh, honey, I wish I was there with you," she soothed.

"Maybe I'll skip class tomorrow and come back to the island tonight."

"No, don't do that. It's too late for you to drive all the way up here."

"But you leave in a little over a week. We have a lot to work out." I desperately wanted to see her. I needed her to reassure me that everything was going to be okay.

Leaning back, I rested my head on the hard, vinyl pillow. After closing my eyes, I thought back to when I'd first met Serena. The chemistry was electric between us, and I was beyond flattered that someone so lovely and talented was interested in me. I let her shower me with praise and opened myself to her attention like a flower opening to the sun in springtime.

CHAPTER THREE

Melissa

I slogged into my bedroom and leaned back on my bed. Was I officially single? Yep, I sure was. I'd been dumped—again.

This time I was truly petrified. I'd never felt so alone. It wasn't like I was twenty-five and single again. I was almost forty-five.

Eastern Washington was the hotbed for conservative Republican politics, and I'd just moved there three months ago. I'm sure I was the only lesbian in a one-hundred-mile radius. Never getting laid again was a real possibility. Forget having a social life. I didn't know anybody yet. All my friends were back on the island.

My best friends lived on Whidbey Island. Why I ever thought it was a good idea to move and take this new job was beyond me.

I tossed and turned all night. I knew my two cats sensed something was wrong as they cuddled up close and didn't leave my side. Unfortunately, the snot from my crying got all over their fur as they feverously tried to clean themselves in the morning.

Lick, lick, lick. I looked over at Sarasota as she thoroughly cleaned her body. It was *O Dark Hundred,* and I knew I wasn't anywhere near the cusp of sleep. So, I emerged from the bed and got ready for work.

†

I knew I looked like hell when I walked into work. I still didn't know my staff all that well because I'd only worked there for three months.

Mary, the most outspoken of the bunch, took one look at me and asked, "Are you okay? You look like hell."

"Yeah, I just had a little trouble sleeping last night. I'm fine."

I might have blamed it on menopause. My memory is a little fuzzy because getting older sucks.

What do you say to a staff you've only known three months? Nope, I'm devastated because my lesbian lover of eight years decided to dump me. Thanks for playing guess what's wrong with the boss this morning.

I plastered a big smile on my face and hibernated in my office for the rest of the day.

Fortunately for me, their previous boss was such an imbecile and not entirely ethical. I only had to show up each day to exceed their expectations. If you're going to change jobs, it's best to pick a place where you have itty-bitty shoes to fill. Pretty much everything I did was a miracle to my attention-starved staff.

My volunteer coordinator, Kim, who was also a social worker, peeked into my office, took one look at my red-rimmed eyes, sat down, and shut the door. At my interview, she was the one who hugged me and begged me to take the job. I felt an instant connection to her, and she was one of the reasons I moved to Republican Land.

"Melissa, Mary mentioned you might be having a tough day. Anything I can help you with?"

Tears welled up in my eyes. I barely held it together. I grabbed a tissue I usually had available for other people who came into my office. Remember, I was the evil HR director like Catbert—at least that's what people assumed about anyone who held this role in an organization.

"Shoot." I wanted to swear, but I didn't because it was one of my rules at work. "I really didn't want to do this. I'm sorry. Is it that obvious?"

"Only to Mary and me. The others are oblivious. You did a good job of fooling everyone else. I'm just exceptional at reading people, and Mary is scary insightful."

I blurted it out before I had a chance to censor myself. "Colette and I split up last night, and I'm having a little difficulty sleeping."

"Shit, I'm sorry. Look, you are the best thing to happen to Kittitas Valley General Hospital. Please tell me you're not going to leave now. I know Ellensburg can be a little conservative, but there are plenty of people here who don't give two shits who you're sleeping with, and I know, with time, you're gonna be okay."

I waved my hand at her as I brushed the tissue against my eyes to keep the mascara from running. "Don't worry, I'm not planning to leave. I just need to find myself a social life. Ellensburg is not really a hotbed for lesbian romance."

"Hey, I've wanted you to come to our house for dinner. Jack is a gourmet cook, and I know he would love to prepare something spectacular for you. Why don't you come to dinner this weekend?"

"Oh, Kim, thanks for the offer, but I might give my best friends on the island a call and visit them for the weekend."

I made it through eight hours without another crying fit and congratulated myself for surviving the first day.

†

I needed to make plans for the weekend because I knew locking myself up in my house and crying all weekend was not healthy. At least, if I intended to cry all weekend, it would be on the shoulders of my best friends, Tori and Janet. I didn't like making the call, but I felt destroyed, and I knew I needed to reach out before thoughts of offing myself came to the surface. Situational depression is what they called it, and I'd been there before—twice.

I took a deep breath and picked up the phone to dial.

Tori answered in her perpetually cheerful tone. She had a spy phone, so she knew who was calling. "Hey, Melissa, what's up?"

I rushed to get it all out at once. "Can I come for the weekend? Colette and I split up."

"What? What the fuck happened?"

Tori never had a problem using the f-word. She swore like a sailor and was proud of her colorful vocabulary.

I breathed in deeply and forced myself to slow my speech. "Colette told me it wasn't working and called it quits last night. I need to be on familiar ground. I don't want to stay at my house, either—memories. I can't bear to sleep there yet."

I'd kept my house on the island because we planned to return in ten years and retire there. I was letting Candie, this little baby dyke who was in school live there for free if she kept up the property and paid the utilities.

"Of course, you can crash here. We'll all go out and have some fun."

"I'm not sure how much fun I'll be, but thanks for letting me come up. I need an anchor right now, and you guys are it."

"Melissa, I'm so sorry you are going through this, and you know that Janet and I will be there for you. Do you want us to call Lanie and Bridget?"

"Yeah, sure, why not? I should get the news out to everyone all at once. Let them join my little pity party."

Lanie, Bridget, and I all became good friends when we worked together at my former hospital. I was closer to Bridget, who was the director of finance, than with Lanie, a nurse. Lanie played in the same band as Colette so I would bet she already knew what had happened. Bridget would be there for me, but I believed Lanie would support me too.

Artists often have *creative differences*. Lanie and Colette had already experienced their fair share of tangles in the past.

Tori was our social coordinator, so I expected she'd plan a social event to keep me distracted. I would have preferred

16

hibernating with the other two introverts, Janet and Bridget, but I knew Tori only meant well, and I didn't want to hurt her feelings.

With the plans locked in place, I braced myself for my next dreaded phone call. I knew I had to tell my family. I tried to stop crying in preparation for the call.

My mom answered, and I managed to get out through my tears what was going on. My dad got on the extension after I was sure my mom had mouthed to him—*I need your help.*

Dad was a retired psychologist and was supposed to be the one to handle broken hearts and major emotional breakdowns. He was the greatest self-professed psychologist that ever walked the earth—not. I knew he meant well, but I didn't want to talk to Dad. I wanted my mom.

I was crying so hard that I wondered if they could understand what I was saying. "I don't know if I can do this. I feel completely alone. Honestly, Mom, I'm seriously considering getting someone to prescribe me a happy pill. I don't think seeing a therapist is going to do it this time."

They had been through this before with me after artist one and artist two dumped me. *Who says good things happen in threes?*

"Do you want us to fly out there?" My dad offered his solution.

I was miserable, and I kinda wanted them to come, but I couldn't bring myself to ask that of them because they lived so far away and were on a fixed income.

"No, that's okay. I'll make an appointment tomorrow with a therapist. I'm sure in a few days, things will be better," I whimpered.

"If you need a prescription for anti-depressant medication, I'm sure your therapist will arrange for you to have that, but you know that's not the answer," Dad offered.

I knew this, but the pain was so acute, I simply wanted it to stop.

"I know, Dad. I know."

"Call us anytime. You know if you need us, we'll be on the next plane," Mom assured me.

"I know, Mom. I love you."

"We love you too."

"Bye, Dad. Bye, Mom."

"Goodnight, honey."

I hung up the phone and nestled in for another night of restless sleep.

†

It was about nine-thirty at night when my phone rang. I looked at the small black device and saw that it was Colette calling. *Shit. I so don't need this right now.*

"Hello."

"Are you okay?"

"Not really. Are you sure this is what you want? Can't we please try to work this out?" I asked.

"I'm so sorry, Melissa. I don't want to hurt you, but I need to do this. I called Tori and Janet tonight, and they told me you would be staying with them this weekend. I'm glad to hear that."

"I can't do this right now. If you're not calling to work things out, please don't call me. I'm barely hanging on by a thread, and your call isn't helping. I need you to leave me alone for a while."

"Okay. Bye, Melissa. I love you."

I hung up the phone and didn't respond to her words. *Why does she have to say she loves me? She's ripping that bandage off—oh so slowly.* I was proud of myself for not asking how she would survive financially. I was on the verge of offering to help her, but I didn't.

I'd been down that road before with artist number two, Tristan. I signed over the truck I had bought her and allowed her to live on the twenty-three-foot boat I owned that sat in a slip in the Oak Harbor Marina. She was a dog person too, so I took care of her dog until she found a way to take care of the one-hundred-fifty-pound mutt.

†

I admit the first time I met Colette I was instantly smitten, but I was with Tristan. Never in my life had I cheated on a girlfriend, and honestly, the thought never crossed my mind when I met Colette. I wasn't wired that way. I could have innocent crushes, but they never went anywhere.

I was training for the Seattle to Portland bike ride, and Lanie's house was a decent distance away, so when Tristan, Lanie, and Colette were at band practice, I offered to bike to the house and meet up with Tristan.

I clomped on the gravel driveway leading to Lanie's place and heard the hauntingly beautiful music floating in the air. Since I didn't want to disturb them in the middle of their practice, I let myself in.

19

Colette was sitting at the keyboards singing a song with a strong social message. It was something about a bell tolling for the sick and the poor. I loved it. It would become a favorite song of mine and one the band always played. Colette had mesmerized me. Her voice was clear with an incredible range. I understood why Lanie and Tristan desperately wanted to find a way for Colette to move to the island and join their band full-time. She would add a lot. She had classic, fine, Italian features, and I knew if they ever played to a lesbian crowd, she'd be a big hit. I didn't know if she was single or not, but that never mattered.

Colette was everything I wasn't. Artists always were. They were passionate and wore their hearts on their sleeve. They weren't afraid of emotion. While I cared deeply about social issues, I'd never found a way to let my voice ring out other than by supporting those causes financially. Colette educated others through song, and it was terribly appealing to listen to her passion come through in her beautiful words.

She was spontaneous and charming, ready to live life to its fullest. That was nearly impossible to resist.

I was a practical Steady Betty. I methodically went to work every day at a job that paid the bills. Oh, and I was good at it. That seemed to matter to me at the time. I didn't exactly hate my job, but it sure didn't feed my soul like music fed Colette's. She wasn't necessarily the practical or responsible sort, and I was. So we worked. She brought the impulsiveness and fun to the relationship, and I brought the resources necessary to enjoy the finer things in life. The very things she didn't like about me were the same attributes that allowed her to live her carefree life.

The music stopped, and I stood awkwardly in the living room with my helmet dangling from my hand. I'm sure I looked a fright with my helmet hair. I'd haphazardly tied my long hair back in a ponytail, but wisps had escaped, and I was pushing them back out of my face.

Tristan and Lanie waved, and I saw Colette's eyes travel up and down my body. She was brazenly checking me out. My face flushed.

Colette hobbled away from her keyboards and stuck her hand out. "You must be Melissa. I'm Colette, the third person in this ragtag band." She had a large boot on her foot.

I'd heard the third member of their band was temporarily off work while she was recuperating from surgery.

"Hi. Nice to meet you." I shook her hand.

"Do you want a drink?" Lanie asked. She had wine sitting on the table next to her.

"No thanks, but I will take some water. I ran out."

"We have about another hour to go. Do you want to wait or are you going to cycle back home?" Tristan asked.

"I'll sit and listen for a little bit, but I'm feeling pretty good, so I might as well get some more miles in. We can grab dinner when you get home." I sat on the couch while Lanie filled my water bottle.

When I left to cycle back home, I caught Colette looking at my legs. I'd been training for months, so I was in tip-top shape. I didn't necessarily think I had a great body, but I had sculpted my legs after hours of cycling on the weekends. Later, she admitted she was indeed ogling my legs that first time we met.

That night, Tristan and I talked about Colette. She asked if it would be possible to let her live with us while she got on

21

her feet. She was going to quit her job and look for work on the island. I said sure. I might have mentioned I thought they sounded good together.

There would never be a U-Haul beginning for Colette and me since she already lived at my house. The way we eventually came together was unusual, to say the least.

CHAPTER FOUR

Colette

I still cared for Melissa. A person doesn't spend eight years with someone and not feel a thing when the relationship ends. She was the stable rock in our partnership. Without even blinking an eye, she paid for most everything. Melissa always encouraged my music and dream to continue my schooling to start a real vocation. We'd planned for that career to contribute to the household bills and set us up for retirement.

I'm not sure why I called Tori and Janet. I suppose a part of me wanted the support of our closest friends. But I had hoped a bigger reason was that I wanted them to reach out to Melissa and help her through our breakup. They'd confirmed what I had already suspected. Melissa was devastated. I should have known her stoic response was merely a facade.

She'd been controlling her emotions for the entire eight years. Why would things be different now?

Tori and Janet, part of the gang we hung with, were our best friends. Everyone in our gang aspired to be like them. They were still madly in love with one another after fifteen years together. They met when they were both in the military and made it through two separations when Janet was stationed somewhere that didn't coincide with Tori's career. Living apart for two years each time didn't affect their rock-solid relationship. Tori finally left active duty and joined the reserves, which gave her more freedom with where she could reside. After Janet retired from the Navy, they'd made Whidbey Island their permanent home.

We owned a boat with them and took a trip every year to Victoria over Labor Day weekend. To be clear, Melissa owned the boat, not me, but since we were a couple, it felt like a four-way partnership.

When I called, Janet wouldn't even get on speakerphone, and Tori's tone was Antarctica frosty. It was clear to me which side of the fence they had landed on. It hurt they wouldn't even consider how this was affecting me or the inevitability of our relationship demise. It had been on a slow spiral for five years.

"Do you have any idea what you've done to Melissa?" Tori asked.

"So, you've taken sides already?"

"I heard about Serena. Candie saw you. You were so engrossed in what you were doing, you didn't even notice. I almost didn't believe her. You're a fucking piece of work." I'd forgotten about going by the house where Candie was staying rent-free in exchange for taking care of the place.

Just another reason everyone would view Melissa as a saint and me as a sinner.

"Oh." I paused and took a big breath. "I don't think you should tell her."

"I'm not lying for you," Tori stated.

"Can you make sure she's okay?" I pulled my glass of wine close.

"She called after Candie broke the news and then I knew it was true. She'll spend the weekend with us. We'll try to help her pull together a thousand pieces of her broken heart that you demolished. I'm sure that someday I'll calm down, but right now, you're a selfish prig. Stay away from her for a while, and for God's sake, don't keep taking advantage of her good nature. Melissa is the one that needs us, not you."

The dial tone reverberated in my ear. Tori was Portuguese and had a hot temper. Perhaps it would soften in time. In the big scheme of things, maybe it wouldn't matter in the long run if all our friends clamored over to team Melissa.

†

I wondered if Tori was right. Was I a selfish prig? I did truly care about Melissa, and I wanted her to have a happy life. I thought I was doing her a favor by ending our anemic relationship.

The largest hurdle was trying to manage the two competing emotions, exhilaration, and guilt. Every time I talked with Serena, I felt like I was on cloud nine. We had danced along the edges of planning our future. Since she lived in Alaska, I was contemplating dropping out of school and moving to the frozen tundra. I was sure I could get a job as a sous chef or maybe break into the music scene. A lot of people didn't realize how much folk music permeated Alaska. They probably had more musicians per capita than any other state. Serena assured me that with my talent, I'd easily be able to make a decent living as an artist. Those words were music to my ears.

We needed to have a serious conversation about logistics before I made any life-altering decisions. Alaska was too far to have a successful long-distance relationship. I'd never wanted anything so bad in my entire life. I was willing to uproot myself for the woman I loved, the woman who was without a doubt my true soulmate, or so I thought at the time.

I picked up my cell phone—the one that Melissa paid for—and called my new girlfriend.

"Hey. What a nice surprise."

"I needed to hear your voice. I suppose I should have known all our friends would rally around Melissa."

"Don't they understand you were slowly dying? You have so much passion and talent. It is never one-sided when a relationship ends. You can't help how you feel. The spark is undeniable between us and nonexistent with you and Melissa."

"Candie saw us."

"Oh shit. Is she going to tell Melissa?"

"I don't think so, but she called Tori and Janet, and they might tell her."

"At least it will be out in the open, and you won't have to hide anything."

"But I lied to her."

"To protect her."

"She won't see it that way. She's big on honesty."

"Sometimes there are good reasons for little white lies."

"I'm not sure this would be categorized as a little white lie. It's not like I told her 'no, your ass doesn't look big in those jeans.'"

"I've seen pictures of Melissa. She's tiny. I doubt her ass ever looked big in anything."

I sighed. "It was just an example of a typical white lie that might be acceptable."

"Oh, right. Hey, when are you coming back to the island?"

"Do you think you could come to Seattle? Melissa is going to the island this weekend to stay with Tori and Janet, and it wouldn't be good to run into her."

"Don't they live in Coupeville?"

"Yeah."

"Well, that's a long way from Hollybrook, and I don't think we'll get out much. Sequestered away in the cabin going from the bedroom to the kitchen sounds delectable. Don't you think?"

My heart skipped a beat. We were at that stage where we couldn't get enough of each other. "Okay, I'll be up after class tomorrow night. Besides, we need to talk about logistics and how we're going to make this work."

I should have picked up on the slight hesitation in her voice when she answered. "Sure, we can do that." My vision of happily ever after burned too brightly for me to see anything else.

CHAPTER FIVE

Melissa

I made it to the weekend and traveled to the island. The whole way there I was deep in thought. When I realized I'd completely spaced out traveling over the Deception Pass Bridge, I kind of freaked out. How was it possible I'd missed that?

Tori answered the door and pulled me into a protective hug. She glanced over at Janet as she opened the door. Janet shook her head. I wasn't sure what was going on, but I would find out later.

Janet pulled me into a hug and whispered in my ear, "Melissa, you are going to survive this."

I pulled away and savagely wiped my tears. I wasn't ready to talk about it.

"So, what's for dinner? It smells heavenly." I peeked into the kitchen and saw something sizzling in a frying pan.

"I made your favorite—crab cakes with my special roasted red pepper sauce. You want a beer or a glass of wine?" Tori asked.

"If you have a bottle of wine open, I'll take a glass. Thanks."

Tori walked over to the counter. I followed her and then sat on one of the stools. She picked up the bottle of wine on the counter, poured a liberal amount, and then handed it to me.

She frowned. "Okay, I'm just gonna say this one thing, and then I'm done. Colette is a fucking bitch."

Janet nodded but didn't say anything.

I started to tear up. "I don't want to talk about it, okay?"

"Sorry," Tori said.

I don't remember everything about that evening, but I did recall completely avoiding the elephant in the room by not talking about anything related to my sad-assed love life.

†

The next morning, after a sleepless night, I threw in the towel and shuffled into the living room. Thank God for Tori, who turned on the automatic coffee maker so there was a freshly brewed cup waiting at six o'clock in the morning. I was staring into space as the master bedroom door opened.

Tori came out rubbing her eyes and had the funniest looking bed head I'd seen in a while. Normally, I would have made fun of it, but I didn't have the energy.

Janet padded out into the living room closely following her lover. Her bed head rivaled Tori's hair.

They both sat on the love seat arranged at a perfect right angle to where I was sitting. Tori looked at Janet, who nodded.

"Melissa, if Colette was seeing someone else, would you want to know?" Tori asked. There was hesitation in her voice.

"*What?*" I screeched.

I'm not stupid, so I knew right away that Colette handed me a line of bullshit and there *was* someone else.

"We're sorry. We didn't know how to tell you, and you didn't want to talk about it last night. I swear we just found out a few days ago."

I gathered my emotions because I wanted to know the details. Just like people rubbernecking at a crash site, I had to hear all the gruesome particulars.

"Please tell me what you know. I asked her, and she flat out lied to my face."

"Candie was at your house when Colette brought her new girlfriend over to pick up a few things. It was obvious they were together. She wasn't hiding anything," Tori explained.

I managed to choke out, "How did she know they were together. Maybe it was only a friend."

"Candie caught them in a passionate embrace—lip lock included."

I crumbled on the couch. Janet came over, sat next to me, and pulled me into an embrace as I cried on her shoulder.

After a few minutes, I lifted my head. I was pissed. Colette was not an early riser, and it was barely six-thirty in the morning.

"Can you guys excuse me for a moment? I need to make a call."

†

We'd started our relationship in a moment of indiscretion on her part. I'm not sure why I was surprised to learn she had cheated on me. Didn't the old saying go something like, once a cheater, always a cheater?

Colette and I had been so good for three years, and she was my longest relationship. I thought the hardest part was over when she'd started back to school and had a sense of purpose. We had our whole future planned out, and we were on track to retire in ten years, maybe fifteen. Then we would head back to the island and our friends. With Colette's salary as a respiratory therapist adding to our nest egg, it would be smooth sailing. She'd come with me when I'd interviewed and supported the decision to move one hundred percent.

I ran downstairs and retrieved my cell phone. I punched the numbers on the device and was amazed I didn't break the damn thing with my ferocity.

After five rings, Colette answered, "Hello."

She sounded groggy, and I was glad I woke her up. "Oh, sorry, did I wake you up?" I asked dripping with sarcasm. "Or did I interrupt your fuckfest with your new lover?"

"Melissa?"

"No, the Easter Bunny. You lied. I asked you point-blank if there was someone else and you said no."

"I thought you were asking if I was leaving because of someone else. That wasn't the reason I left you."

"How long and don't lie. I think after eight years, I deserve the truth."

Colette sighed. "Since the Fourth of July. I met her when I worked that weekend at Hollybrook. We connected like I've never experienced before with anyone else. She's my soulmate."

"Are you fucking kidding me? That was two weeks ago. You left me for someone you met two weeks ago. We have eight years."

"She's Claire's daughter, and she was visiting from Alaska. She gets me, but I told you I didn't leave you for Serena. I left because we don't connect anymore."

Claire was Collete's boss at Hollybrook and a good friend of hers. With a fleeting thought, I wondered what Claire thought of this new development with her daughter.

"You're a fucking liar and a cheat." I punched the end button and tossed the phone on the bed.

When I'd gone to one of the family dinners, the founders of Hollybrook hosted for the staff, everyone had talked about Claire's drop-dead gorgeous daughter, but Colette never had time to meet her before July. Coincidentally, Serena was gay and, apparently, Colette's soulmate.

I was fuming. Colette used me this whole time because she needed financial stability in her life. I figured now that she didn't need her "Sugar Mamma," she could find her true soulmate—and it wasn't me.

†

I clumped back upstairs and sat down heavily on the couch. Janet and Tori merely looked at me.

"I say we eat breakfast, laze around until noon when we can legitimately start drinking, and then get toasted without being labeled raging alcoholics."

This was Tori's answer to my current predicament, and I decided what the hell—it would beat crying all day.

I folded myself into a protective little ball on the couch and read. As a fellow introvert, I'm pretty sure Janet understood. I didn't want to process anything at the time because I had to let things fester inside.

Tori kept looking over at me, and I knew she was wondering when I would tell her about the phone call, but Janet simply shook her head, so Tori left me alone.

I figured I might as well read a book—one about someone else's shitty love life. At least, in the end, I knew it was all going to work out. That was why I read all those sappy lesbian love stories because there was always a happy ending—at least in the ones I selected. They were amazingly instructional regarding new ways to have sex. Of course, I didn't exactly need that right now because I was probably never having sex again. My sex life was sadly over at age forty-five.

The only thing that kept me from nodding off due to lack of sleep was the fact that the book I was reading was particularly good. It had a fair amount of especially steamy parts.

Janet put on a relaxing CD, and for the first time in six days, I wasn't ready to slit my wrists. I hadn't turned a corner quite yet, but I wasn't at the bottom of the well, either.

Glancing at the clock, I noticed it was eleven thirty. I could tell Tori was getting antsy as she began to squirm around on the loveseat. She'd been reading a magazine, and her inner extrovert was dying to start a conversation.

I laid down my book and looked at Tori. "All right, let's pack up the alcohol and head to the beach."

"Awesome. I'll call Candie. I know she'll want to come join us. Should I call Lanie and Bridget?" Tori jumped up and headed into the kitchen.

"Nah, I'm sure it will be tough for them with the kids," I told her.

Lanie and Bridget had three kids. We were all their adopted godmothers since the whole group of us were at the home birth of their first child. With the doula and midwife, there were thirteen women at the blessed event. We liked to refer to our little passel as the coven. Two years later, they received a big surprise when they found out Lanie was pregnant with twins. She wasn't able to have them at home, so I took care of Corbin, their first, while Lanie had a C-section. I couldn't imagine having three toddlers at the age of forty-five, but Lanie and Bridget were incredible moms.

I got up from the couch and stretched.

Janet stood up, came over, put her arm around my shoulder and whispered in my ear, "I know you don't need this shit right now, but be careful because Candie has a huge crush on you, and she'll probably bust a gut to be the shoulder you need to cry on."

"Great, just what I need a baby dyke fifteen years my junior, figuring out that her Jehovah's Witness upbringing might not be all that much fun anymore. Especially now, considering she likes girls."

"Sorry, Melissa, I thought you needed to know," Janet said.

"Thanks, but tell her I'm not in the mood for Red and Blackie right now."

Before going to my friend's place of refuge, I had dropped off the dogs at my house on the island. I'd asked Candie if she could take care of them and she had agreed to do me that favor. The house had a large fenced yard, and I couldn't very well leave them in Cle Elum unattended for the weekend. It was time for another call to my ex.

I punched the button on my cell phone and made a second call to Colette.

Not saying hello, I started right in. "You need to figure out something for Red and Blackie because I can't keep dragging them to the island with me on the weekends. It's not fair to hoist them off on Candie."

I was still pissed, so I figured she didn't deserve any formal niceties from me like hello or goodbye.

She didn't argue. "Okay, Melissa. Can you give me a week to arrange something?"

"Yeah, sure." I closed my phone and ended the call without a goodbye.

I turned to look at Tori and noted her raised eyebrows. Neither Tori nor Janet had ever seen me be rude before. I was the kind of person people walked all over. Maybe being dumped a third time helped me grow a backbone.

Tori grabbed her beach bag, a cooler filled with alcohol, and headed for the door. "Time to soak up the sun and get toasted."

†

35

I looked out over the frigid blue-green water of the Puget Sound as the tide slapped against the rocks in a playful rhythmic dance. The beach was not your typical beach, but instead, a combination of beige sand, rocks, and pieces of driftwood placed haphazardly over the seaweed and sand. The chaotic nature of the beach reminded me of my life.

I sat heavily on one of the pieces of driftwood, and Janet took a seat to my right while Candie sat to my left.

Tori pulled out a bottle of Mike's Hard Lemonade and wordlessly handed it to me. "So, how is the new job? Are you enjoying it? Do you miss us?"

"Job's good, but yes, you have no idea how much I miss you guys. I can't believe I moved to 'Nowheresville.' Of course, I'm totally second guessing my decision now."

"Sorry, but for what it's worth, I think you made the right decision. Doctor Z is still as crazy as ever, and I'm not sure I'm gonna make it." Tori looked over at me.

Tori was the community relations director at my old hospital, and she supported the other candidate along with me. I suspected Doctor Z was making her life miserable right now like I was sure he would have done to me.

"Wait him out, Tor. I know you can hang on, and you'll drive him crazy while doing it," I remarked.

"Have you met anyone to hang with in cowboy land?" Tori asked.

"My staff is great, but no, not really."

"Are you still doing stuff with your biking group?" Candie asked.

"Yes, that will probably be my only social activity until I find others to hang with, or I can always come back to the island every weekend."

"Absolutely. You are always welcome back here," Tori said.

"Don't worry. I'm not gonna crash here every weekend. You guys have your own life. I'm sure I'll bounce back in a few weeks." I shrugged.

"Melissa, you know we love you, and we will always be here for you," Janet added.

"I know."

"Look, I'm not the best one to give this advice, because I'm sure if I was in your shoes, I'd turn into a hermit, but I don't think you should do that. Being a recluse is not healthy, and I know that's what you're tempted to do." Janet shifted her gaze to meet mine.

I looked down and didn't answer. I didn't want to lie to my friends because that was exactly what I was planning to do.

Tori paced in front of me as she blurted out, "You should sign up for Match.com." Janet glared at her. "I'm not suggesting you should start dating. I just think it would be good to connect with lesbians who might live closer. It's nice to have people to bike or hang with."

I looked up at her, knowing she meant well, so I placated her. "Yeah, maybe I will."

Candie smiled at me and said, "Good for you. You go, girl. You should be careful though because if you make a connection, all those single lesbians will be all over you. Melissa, you're smart, beautiful, and stable. You are a fabulous catch. I can't believe Colette was stupid enough to let you go."

"There was no letting go on her part—it was more like the big dump. I need to find an artist-free zone. Whatever I do, we need to make a pact you will not let me fall for another artist. Deal?"

We all extended our right hands into a circle, did the team sport salute, and all three of them shouted in unison, "Deal."

Tori was jumping up and down like Tigger. In fact, Tigger was her favorite Winnie the Pooh character. Go figure. I wasn't sure what character I was—probably Eeyore at that moment, but I wasn't normally like that. I suppose my current frame of mind was like the situational depression my dad so fondly labeled—being Eeyore was situational Pooh.

As Tori bounced on the balls of her feet, she exclaimed, "We're gonna set you up tonight on Match. It'll be so much fun."

I grumbled, "Yeah, as much fun as a colonoscopy."

"I'll bet you get a ton of winks in the first hour."

"Whoa. Back that love truck up. I do not want to date anyone right now. I only want people to bike with because none of you losers are cyclists, and once a month with my bike group is not going to keep my melancholy at bay. On second thought, can we please skip the Match idea?"

"No, no way. I promise I'll set it up so everyone knows you only want people to hang with, not fuck." Tori grinned.

Janet glared at Tori. "Babe, you need to leave her alone. If she doesn't want to do it, let it be."

"Okay." Tori gave me her pouty face and then looked down at her feet.

I gave in because they were my best friends, and I didn't want to disappoint them or overburden them with my grief.

"It's okay, Janet. I'll do it."

I'd already lost weight, so when I finished my second Mike's, I was severely buzzed. My five-foot-six, one-hundred-thirteen-pound frame, didn't allow me to drink too much anymore. It wasn't like I could ever drink very much, anyway.

I decided puking up my breakfast at age forty-four was not in the cards, so I grabbed a bottle of water. Too bad—I was starting to feel a little less depressed. I'd always been a happy drunk.

We continued to gossip about people I knew at my old hospital, and it took my mind off my current broken heart.

I decided it was time to let go, and come Monday, I'd take Colette off my insurance and close all our joint credit cards—the ones she'd used, and I paid for. Until this morning, I was holding out for reconciliation when Colette came to her senses, but with her new hottie, that clearly wasn't happening.

After another hour or so, I started back on the Mike's because a slight buzz was okay with me. It was deadening the pain, and for the moment, I wanted my liquid happy pill. I didn't get sloppy drunk, but I wasn't exactly sober, either.

When we headed back to Tori and Janet's place, I was giggling and ready to put silly things on the Match.com site.

†

Everyone but Janet staggered into the house. Someone had to be ready with the aspirin and water when we sobered up.

Tori fired up the computer and got on the Match.com site.

39

She started asking questions, but she didn't give me time to answer. "Okay, Melissa, your build is… slight and athletic. You're forty-four, right?" I nodded. "No religious preference, right?"

She didn't wait for me to answer and checked the boxes.

"Definitely a cat person, no dogs, right?" She looked over at me.

"Well, I prefer cats, but some dogs are okay if they're well behaved, I guess. Wait, why are you answering all these questions? I'm not looking for my next wife. I only want a biking companion. It shouldn't matter what I like and don't like regarding pets or anything else."

Tori waved her hand at me. "No worries. I know you well enough to answer. Some of these questions are required. I'm only following the form. Ooh, here's a place to upload a picture. I have a perfect shot. I'll just cut Colette out of the picture."

I groaned. "This is a big mistake. Janet, you better hand me another Mike's. I'm starting to sober up, and we can't have that, now can we?"

I stood up, looked over Tori's shoulder, and gasped at what she was writing.

I'm kind of an introvert, so I'm not sure what to write. This is a whole new thing for me, but if anyone is interested in biking or hanging out as friends, that's what I'm looking for. Since I recently got out of a long-term relationship, I'm not ready for anything but meeting some women to hang out with, especially if you are an avid cyclist like me.

Even though what she had written was accurate, I sounded kind of pitiful. I figured that might be a good thing because I wouldn't have to respond to anyone. Surely, no one in their right mind would give my post a second look.

I giggled because the fourth Mike's was kicking in now. "Hey, put in there I'm phenomenal in bed because introverts spend all our time researching new sex positions. Oh, and since we don't talk much, our tongues are extra talented because all our focus goes into using them properly."

The rest of my merry band of accomplices giggled. Thankfully, Tori knew if she put that on the site, I would never forgive her.

Tori's fingers were flying over the keyboard, and as she punched the last key, she exclaimed, "Done. Your username is *Melissacycle,* and your password is *Colettesabitch.*"

"Funny."

I spent the rest of the weekend with Tori, Janet, and Candie. I even managed to laugh a little. In two short weeks, I would turn forty-five. At that moment, I felt every single day of the forty-five years on the planet. I felt old and used.

†

Tori and Janet mentioned they would be out of town for my birthday, so Candie said she would come to Cle Elum and cook me a birthday dinner. I didn't have the energy to refuse her offer, and a small part of me was grateful I wouldn't be alone, even if I were entering the danger zone. I needed to be clear that we would only ever be friends. Our life experiences weren't even in the same decade, so it would never be a match made in heaven. Candie was a sweet girl, but that's exactly how I saw her—a girl, not a woman.

It was back to work on Monday.

CHAPTER SIX

Colette

When the phone rang at six in the morning, I rolled over and tried to grab it before Serena woke up. We'd spent half the night making love, and I was sure she wouldn't want to wake up yet. I could still smell the evidence of our passion.

"Hello?"

"Oh, sorry, did I wake you up?" Melissa asked dripping with sarcasm. "Or did I interrupt your fuckfest with your new lover?"

Before I answered, "Melissa," I had the unkind thought how she hadn't interrupted us, but I was sure not going to tell her that.

The conversation went downhill from there. It didn't end on a positive note, but at least everything was out in the open now.

Serena rolled over and opened her bleary eyes. With her hair tousled, I couldn't help my instant reaction. I wanted to curl up inside of her again. I was wide awake from the phone call and now from her catlike movements that seemed to define sensuality.

"Sounds like Tori and Janet told her about us. You don't look too upset about it."

I smiled. "I should be, but you're very distracting in the morning, looking all... oh, I don't know... like you've had a wonderful night of passion but are ready for round two. It's also a relief. I knew lying wasn't the right thing to do."

Serena reached for me. "Come here. The right thing to do is live a full, happy life and to engage in some naughty calisthenics with me."

The guilt took backstage to the ecstasy.

†

I wasn't sure how Claire felt about her daughter and me, but she was gracious when I asked about using the kitchen to cook brunch for both of us. We both needed the sustenance after the long night of unbridled passion.

Serena had somehow found a sex shop and bought a few toys. I wasn't exactly uncomfortable in the morning, but I definitely felt the aftereffects. Muscles and parts of my body that hadn't had a lot of action in the past three years had come to life in an explosion of immense pleasure.

I was humming one of my songs and flipping the stuffed French toast in the pan when Serena came up behind me and kissed my neck. "Mmm, that smells almost as good as you taste." Her tongue ran up the edge of my ear and then she nibbled the bottom before taking a step back.

"Is there anything I can do to help you?"

I shook my head. "Not really, unless you want to pour the coffee and put it on that tray? This is almost ready." I pointed to the tray without the food.

The plates, napkins, and cutlery were on one tray, and the bacon, syrup, and fruit were on the other, waiting for the French toast. It was a little crowded, but I hoped it would all fit so we wouldn't need to make a second trip back to the cabin with our breakfast.

The final piece of toast was a beautiful golden brown. I pulled out the stack from the oven that I was keeping warm and flipped the final slice on the top. After moving around the rest of the items so the warm plate would fit, I picked up the tray and gestured with my head for Serena to carry the other one.

"Do you mind grabbing the tray with the carafe of coffee and plates, and then we can head back down to the cabin and replenish our energy."

"Fantastic. I'm famished and can't wait to dig in. A woman who can cook, sing, and fuck all night. I've hit the lottery."

I didn't like the way she'd described our night of lovemaking. To me, our nights of passion were spiritual experiences, and that didn't equate with fucking, which sounded more like scratching an itch. Nothing romantic about that. Although, I had to admit, sometimes calling out for someone to fuck me harder did ratchet up the experience.

I was, however, in a bit of a quandary as tiny hints that life might not turn out as I'd initially envisioned began to pile up.

†

Leaning back on the headboard, Serena rubbed her stomach. "That was orgasmic. I'm so full, I can't move."

I picked up the plate she'd placed on the nightstand after she'd finished eating and took it into the other room where the remnants of our breakfast lingered. There were mere crumbs now. After re-entering the room, I climbed on top of the bed and scooched my body next to her. "I'm going to miss you so much when you go back to Alaska. My heart already aches with the thought that we don't know when we'll see each other again."

She turned her head. "Come to Alaska. I know you'd love it there. I was serious about the music scene. We could form our own band. I know a drummer…"

Jubilation. That was exactly the right thing for her to say. "Do you really mean that? I only have one more quarter of school, but the thought of not seeing you for three months is enough to send me over the edge. Maybe, down the road, I can figure out a way to finish school."

"I have a small place you can crash, and we can see where it goes."

It wasn't exactly an undying declaration of love or a firm offer for a future together, but I plucked at the tiny thread and pulled. I should have known when I did that, everything would unravel. Maybe not today, but it wouldn't take long.

"It might take me a month or so to wrap things up. I'm not sure what I'll do with the dogs…"

"Melissa will keep them for you, won't she? She has two houses, and both are fenced. It shouldn't be a big deal, right?"

I bit the bottom of my lip. Guilt re-emerged. "Maybe I can ask Candie if she'd be willing to look after them. Melissa isn't a dog person, and I already told her I would figure something out. Eventually, we can find a way to have them shipped."

"I guess we'll have to figure something out. My place is a little small for two large dogs, but I get that they're important to you."

Her nonchalant afterthought of my babies should have brought my raging feelings to a screeching halt, but no such luck. A small part of me wanted to replay our beginning because I had just felt the tiniest shift. It wasn't enough to stop me from imagining Serena and me looking out on the beautiful Alaska landscape, happy in our knowledge that we were made for each other.

CHAPTER SEVEN

Melissa

A reluctant journey back to three weeks ago...
I got back to my little house late on Sunday after the
three-hour drive, and I started to do what I normally did
when left to my own devices. I obsessed over the fact that I
hadn't seen it coming. The affair had started on the long July
Fourth weekend.

I kicked my shoes off into the closet. Already, there
were black marks against the wall, and I knew I should stop
doing that. Sarasota and Freud were both cuddled up with
one another, but the minute I climbed into bed after grabbing
several tissues, they both bookended me. Freud took up his
favorite position on my left side. He was persnickety. Never
choosing the left side, Sarasota settled next to my right side.

I don't care what anyone else says, cats are far from
aloof. Dogs may be man's best friend, but cats are a lesbian's

perfect choice of a confidant, right along with either a tub of ice cream or a bottle of wine. They know when you're in pain and take it upon themselves to stick to you like glue.

I forced myself to relive three weeks earlier when Tori and Janet came for a visit because Colette had to work. I had to find that elusive clue to the impending implosion that was my life.

†

The wind was blowing hard again, and I finally understood all those comments about Ellensburg. Apparently, spring and summer were notorious for intense winds. The temperature was in the seventies, but it felt like fifties. We were trying to decide what to do besides go to the hokey parade in Cle Elum.

Janet was a former meteorologist and explained the phenomenon of the valley. She gave details about the Cascade Mountains and how they created a weakness called the Stampede Gap. In the summer, the pressure was higher on the west side and lower over the basin in eastern Washington. As those pressure differences increased during the day, the temperatures rose on the east side of the mountains. That air accelerated over the weak gap and created the wind patterns. Blah, blah, blah. I knew we were in for another exceptionally windy day. It had already started.

I was showing Janet the rock with the famous Ellensburg Blue surrounding the crystal center. Lanie found the precious rock in my backyard about a month before when she and Bridgett were visiting with the kids. It was such a good-sized specimen, it had an estimated worth of several thousand dollars. Janet, like myself, was a rock hound, so we decided to go to the location I'd heard was a likely spot to find another rock like the one I held in my hand for her inspection.

We all had jackets on to keep the wind from causing a chill. Onlookers from the road must have been busting a stitch as they watched three middle-aged women slipping and sliding up a waterfall of rocks on the side of the road.

We picked our way excitedly through the treasures hidden among the common pebbles and compressed slate. The old coal mine shafts were still present at the top of the hill. A local told me about the secret spot across from a bend in the road where the Yakima River glistened in the sunshine. He'd mentioned something about a rock slide that had uncovered the precious gems deposited in the glacier on the mountainsides a millennium ago.

"Is this one?" Janet held up a small blue rock.

I tried to carefully crabwalk my way to take a closer look. Instead, I ended up crawling over to her none too gracefully. Accepting the tiny stone from Janet, I turned it over in my hand. "Yeah, I think so. You should take it to a jeweler to confirm."

Janet chuckled. "Nah, I just want a little token of our visit to your neck of the woods."

"I feel like a fucking crab," Tori grumbled. "How much longer do you think we'll be here?" She flopped on her back and took in the sun's rays. "I'll sunbathe until you nerds are done."

Tori wasn't a rock hound or science geek like Janet and me. She was biding her time until we decided on a place to eat. "We can head to lunch anytime you want," I offered.

"How about we leave in a half an hour? I want to find at least one more. This is like a treasure hunt. I'm having a blast," Janet said.

"I should have brought some booze," Tori answered.

"Too bad Colette couldn't be here. I know she would appreciate this."

"She would. She was thrilled when Lanie found the rock. She wanted to do a thorough search to see if we could find any more. I keep looking, but so far, no go."

That reminded me I hadn't called her yet, but I didn't want to be rude to our guests, so I decided to call her after we'd all turned in for bed.

It had been hard on Colette when they'd essentially laid her off from Hollybrook after the recession diminished the eleven-million-dollar trust to dangerous levels. They weren't sure they could afford a full-time chef for the writers. Whenever they called, she went running and picked up per diem shifts here and there. It was her perfect job. She was in nirvana among the other writers. In addition to being a talented musician, Colette was quite the writer. She was unpublished, but that didn't make her any less gifted. It seemed artists had a certain language only they understood.

†

Janet and Tori had settled in for the night, so I grabbed a bottle of water and my cell phone and headed into my tiny master bedroom. Sarasota and Freud were cuddled together in their usual spot. I hated to disturb them, but I was exhausted after entertaining my friends for the entire day. As an introvert, it took everything out of me, even though they were my best friends.

I crawled under the covers and selected Colette's cell phone number. It was late, but I hoped she was up. I knew she would talk with the writers after dinner sometimes, so I thought there was a good chance I would catch her before she turned in. They let her sleep in the bedroom next to the library. I'd crashed there with her once when she'd invited me to watch the meteor shower. It wasn't a happy memory.

Somehow a mosquito was trapped in the room and continued to buzz around us. The sound overwhelmed me in the quiet of the room. Since Hollybrook was out in the sticks, it was as quiet as death there. This set off my over-the-top phobia of insects of the flying variety and caused a full-blown meltdown.

Colette couldn't understand why I lay shaking under the covers and didn't get one ounce of sleep. Her irritation was evident when she yelled at me to go to sleep. I thought she should be a bit more sympathetic. I knew it wasn't rational. Phobias never are. I had told her the story of its origins. That should have been enough for her to accept this idiosyncrasy.

I thought it was perfectly logical. When you had spent time stuck in a roach-infested bedroom lying on the floor, watching hundreds of the nasty little buggers through the dim light as they crawled all over the floors and ceiling, it was certain to cause nightmares. I was only six and stayed awake all night long with the covers pulled up hoping they wouldn't fall on me or crawl over my body. It left a lasting impression and a nasty phobia that never went away.

Colette's cell phone went to voice mail after four rings. I was disappointed, but I figured I could call again in the morning and catch her before she prepared their brunch.

"Hey, it's me. I guess you already turned in for the night. I'll call tomorrow. Hope you had fun today. We found some more Ellensburg Blues. Not like the one we have, but Janet was thrilled. Goodnight." I left the voice message and was fast asleep as soon as Freud snuggled up with me and started purring.

At the time, I thought nothing of it. The big events in my life never came with warnings, and this was no exception. Clues, perhaps—but I needed big flashing red lights, or I was oblivious.

CHAPTER EIGHT

Colette

Three weeks ago…

Claire had been trying to get me to meet her daughter for years. Finally, Serena was visiting over the Fourth of July. She was living in Alaska and needed a break. Hollybrook was the perfect place to visit for peace and relaxation.

Every evening after I'd served all the writers at the retreat, we would gather in the common room and talk about everything under the sun. I always brought my guitar, and when they asked, I'd play a few songs I'd written and recorded.

Hollybrook is an old dairy farm looking out over Useless Bay that a visionary benefactor transformed into a women's writers retreat. It was the perfect place to work because an amazing assortment of women focusing and talking about

53

their art had blessed my humble existence. As a musician, I fed off their energy.

When Serena walked into the kitchen that first night, I felt my heart quicken. She was stunning in her low-rise jeans and a tight T-shirt. She had the kind of natural beauty I was sure everyone envied. I smiled and greeted her.

"You must be Serena." I held out my hand, but she pulled me into a hug. It felt nice to have someone hold me so close again.

"Colette," she whispered. "My mom talks about you all the time. I was so excited to meet you after I heard your CD," she gushed.

"I brought my guitar," I mumbled as she stepped back from the hug. I wanted to play for her. I wanted to touch her intimately with my music so that she would stay connected to me. Her energy wove its way into my body, and I experienced the passion that was lacking in my relationship with Melissa. It was intoxicating, and I wanted the feeling to continue.

"Awesome. I brought mine too. Maybe we can jam later."

"Okay." That sounded good. After dinner, I figured I could stay in the guest room next to the common area. We would have plenty of time to jam and get to know each other. I wanted to get to know this gorgeous creature.

She was looking intently at me, and a slow sexy smile appeared on her face. "You are entirely too cute for my own good. Too bad you're taken, because I could definitely fall for you."

I was beyond flattered, and that was all it took. There was this amazing connection, and consequences be damned. I was intent on exploring those feelings that had been dormant for so long.

†

We always served the writers wine with the special dinner I prepared for them. The energy before dinner was electrifying with the buzz of conversation. Serena joined the group, and not only was she beautiful, but witty and intelligent too. She was a musician and shared her depth of emotion in the words of her songs—just like I did.

Music is poetry with a beat. It must have been kismet I'd brought my guitar with me that night. Karma came knocking on my door very shortly after that. Karma is a vengeful bitch.

I kept looking in Serena's direction, and she caught my furtive glances. As she stretched her long, lean, form and stood, I saw her eyeball my guitar. It was propped up against the wall in the small library adjacent to the dining room where all the writers were gathered. "So, is that yours?"

I nodded as I continued to cut up the vegetables for the stir-fry. "Yeah, I don't know why I brought it. I usually don't have time to play after my shift."

"When my mom told me you were quite a musician, I asked her for your CD. I meant what I said before. I'd love to jam with you tonight—after you're done with your shift, of course." Serena smiled, and it transformed her face into something so compelling I couldn't look away. She lazily made her way to the large kitchen with more gadgets than a cooking store. It was a chef's paradise.

I handed her a glass of wine and poured myself a healthy amount. I'd been having a glass or two with the writers even though I knew what Melissa would say. Honestly, I didn't think a glass of wine now and then constituted falling from the wagon, but it certainly had been a huge cause of disagreement between us. When Melissa gave me that look, I felt like a naughty five-year-old. I hated that she controlled everything, including how I felt about drinking that glass of wine. I tried to help her understand this, but it didn't work. In her mind, I was an alcoholic who had lied to her. Technically, she was correct about the lying, but the jury was still out on the alcoholic part as far as I was concerned.

Serena didn't leave the kitchen area, and I felt her scrutinize me while I worked. She leaned casually against the counter, sipping from her wine. "This is good. Mom always pulls out the cheap shit. I guess she figures I'm not worthy of the good stuff the writers appear to get."

"I pick out the wine I think will pair best with the meal."

A sudden heat crawled up my body as she moved around the counter and stood within a foot of where I'd tossed the ingredients into the deep round wok. Apparently, Serena had a very small need for personal space. She made an overt sniffing noise and brushed against my shoulder as she peered into the pan. "Mmm, smells delish."

I swallowed hard and wondered if I was catching a whiff of her pheromones. She had a clean citrus scent mixed with something I hadn't smelled in a long time. It was the scent of a woman. I could smell her arousal—or was it mine—as I shifted uncomfortably.

"Do I make you nervous? You seem unsettled," she said.

"No, of course not. I figured someone who comes from Alaska, with all the wide-open area, would have a much larger bubble."

She took a step back and laughed. "Sometimes I like to see how people will react when I get too close. Social psychology has always fascinated me. Besides, you're adorable when you're rattled."

I let out the breath I was holding after she spun on her heels and left the room to join the writers again. I tried to ignore them so I could finish what I was doing and serve dinner at a reasonable time, but I kept getting distracted as I heard her unique laugh rise above the chatter.

†

While I was finishing the dishes after dinner, I heard the soft strumming of a guitar. When I pushed up on my toes to look out the window, I saw Serena's head slightly bent as she played the various chords. It was a relaxing piece, and she hadn't started to sing yet, but as a musician, I registered the difficulty of the composition. Serena wasn't simply a play around the campfire guitarist.

The sweet sound of her voice floated in the air. I imagined the sound was like a butterfly lifting its wings and traveling from flower to shrub looking for something interesting to land on.

I hurried through my nightly chores, not because it was a forty-five-minute drive to Melissa's house on the island, but because I intended to join Serena and jam with her as she had suggested. The house on the island was where I crashed when I picked up extra shifts at Hollybrook, but tonight, I had already decided to stay in the bedroom next to the library.

Candie was the caretaker for the house on the island because Melissa wanted to keep it for when we retired. Although Melissa and I lived together and had exchanged rings, she was cautious about putting the house in both our names. I knew a previous lover had burned her before, and I never pushed the issue. Why would I? She practically paid for everything. My contributions were miniscule and thus the feeling that it wasn't a partnership at all. She controlled the money, our plans for the future, even the placement of the furniture. I suppose I was a kept woman.

I shook my head in an attempt to loosen those bitter thoughts and sent them flying in every direction.

With all the dishes done and everything put away in the kitchen, I grabbed my guitar from the library and slung it over my shoulder so that my hands were free to grab a bottle of wine and two glasses. After sticking the bottle under my arm, I carefully maneuvered the glasses in my right hand and then turned the handle to the door. I felt like a juggler in the circus. If I hadn't weighed myself down with everything I wanted to carry outside, I would have skipped out to the bench that Serena was sitting on.

"Mind if I join you?" I set down the glasses and then slipped the guitar off and set it against the bench.

"Please do. I was hoping to entice you out tonight. I see you brought the liquid courage." She reached for the bottle of wine. "I don't think my teeth are strong enough to bite through glass, though. Should I go inside and get a corkscrew?"

Liquid courage. Was that what I had unintentionally done? I'd often behaved badly in the past and used the excuse I was drunk and didn't know what I was doing. It's

how Melissa and I first got together. I'd made a play for her
ex-girlfriend, and we'd kissed. That was the beginning of the
end for Melissa and Tristen, the drummer in my old band.

Turns out she wasn't even interested in me, but she did
admit to Melissa she was in love with our lead singer, Lanie.
Unfortunately, Tristen had cemented the demise of their
relationship when the secret came out.

One night, we were all watching a television show.
Melissa had invited me to live with her and Tristan during
my recovery from foot surgery. The silly show started a
debate over whether not sharing a truth was a lie or not. Soon
after, the small prompt had Tristen singing like a canary
because the guilt was eating her up.

Even though Lanie, who was now up to her ass chasing
around twins in her spare time, never returned her affections,
Tristan and Melissa hadn't made it over the typical lesbian
drama. I had swooped in and became the shoulder for
Melissa to cry on. Melissa was so hauntingly beautiful that
night as she lay open and vulnerable. Over our eight years
together, she was rarely anything but stoic and composed. I
kissed her that night, and she let me. I think she needed to
feel like someone wanted her that night and I did. What an
incestuous group we were. All good friends who had
somehow managed to forgive each other for our
transgressions.

Shortly after the breakup between Tristan and Melissa,
those good friends did an intervention with me. They were
worried about my bruises and how I'd started puking up
blood. Melissa was the primary spokesperson and quite
bluntly informed me that she believed I was an alcoholic, and
if I didn't quit drinking, I was likely to spiral out of control. I

quit drinking for three full years. When I started drinking again, and Tristan tried to tell Melissa, she stoutly refused to believe her until the evidence was overwhelming, and I finally copped to the truth. The lie had hung between us, acting as an impenetrable barrier that never quite dissolved. We'd had five full years of rocky road without the deliciousness of the famous ice cream. There was nothing sweet about couples therapy, lies, and the slow choking of our former love and passion.

I convinced myself a little wine wouldn't be the end of the world. Pulling the corkscrew from my pocket, I presented it to Serena like a precious gift. "As a former Girl Scout, you should know we're always prepared."

Serena raised her eyebrow. "Ah, but what exactly are you prepared for?"

There was no question in my mind Serena was flirting with me, and I was giving it right back.

"Does anyone really prepare for this sort of thing?" I answered. "I'm not sure illicit affairs are covered in the Girl Scout handbook."

"Well, hells bells, I'm impressed. No beating around the bush with you. Good thing, because there are far more exciting things to do in the bush." Serena tipped back her head and laughed at her own joke. "God, that was awful, wasn't it?"

I shook my head. My heart was pounding so loud in my chest with a mix of both excitement and anxiety. Was I going to cheat on Melissa with Serena? I pointed to one of the glasses sitting innocently on the bench. "Better fill that to the brim for me."

"Happy to, after I get the wine open."

She proceeded to expertly pull the cork from the bottle, then filled a glass to within a quarter of an inch from the rim. I carefully accepted the liquid courage and took a large gulp. Wine isn't meant to be gulped, but I wasn't nearly tipsy enough for what was about to transpire.

Serena gave me a puzzled look but didn't comment. She filled her glass, a little less full and raised it to the dark sky. The moon gave just enough light for the reflection to shimmer off the wine. A full moon can be surprisingly bright.

"Here's to always being prepared."

†

Serena was an easy person to fall in love with, or after considerable hindsight, I suppose it might have been intense lust. Her boldness and charisma made her an unstoppable force of nature. I suspect that whatever Serena wanted, she got. Unfortunately, that same spontaneity and take-charge personality came with a decidedly less charming side. When something is too good to be true, I've learned it normally is.

The bottle of wine sat on the ground with a mere droplet of liquid at the bottom mocking me. I knew I shouldn't have finished the bottle with Serena because, in the back of my mind, a niggling of truth tried hard to surface. I kept insisting I could handle a couple of glasses of wine without harm, but tonight, I'd had more than a few and was most definitely drunk.

Her talent as a musician spoke to me, and as we played together, harmonized, and moved into sync, one I'd not experienced with anyone in a long time, I fell for her and tumbled down that path hard. Wearing my admiration like a badge of honor, Serena easily saw my veneration.

I'd played her one of my best songs about a dream lover who comes to life, and she'd asked me if I would teach her the song so she could sing it with me. I was thrilled.

Once we'd finished singing the song together, she admitted, "I have a confession to make. After my mom gave me your CD, I played it over and over again so many times I've memorized the words and music. Singing the song with you is the single most thrilling experience as a musician I've ever known. Frankly, I'm surprised you aren't touring around the world with fans screaming your name."

I looked at her in shock, and that's when Serena set her guitar aside and gently removed mine to place it next to hers. They looked like two lovers, side by side, gazing at the stars.

I knew this was the point of no return. If I accepted her kiss, my destiny would be set in stone. I couldn't undo the betrayal to Melissa if I allowed the pull of her lips.

When she stood, and her hand seductively skated over my arm and then grabbed my hand to pull me to a standing position, I let her. When her lips connected with mine and her tongue sought entry, I eagerly welcomed the velvety feeling as she kissed me with a passion I hadn't experienced in an awfully long time.

We broke apart, and Serena whispered, "I want to make love to you so bad right now that if you say no, I don't think I'll ever recover from the rejection."

"I won't say no." I'd already violated my vows with the kiss; following the natural path to her bed was simply a matter of walking down the dirt track to the cottage she was staying at.

†

The anticipation and excitement of imagining her hands and mouth on my body were mere seconds away as we'd both quickly removed and tossed our clothes on the floor beside the queen-sized bed in the cabin. I don't know if the illicit nature of what we were about to do enhanced my arousal; that was certainly a possibility. Regardless of the reason, I was a volcano about to explode.

Her grin grew as she pushed me onto the bed and climbed on top. The moan or groan slipped out as her fully naked body melded with my own. She rocked on top of me, and her kisses became more frantic. We moved together up and down, and I was so close before she pulled me into a position where she could touch me from behind, teasing mercilessly as she barely reached the edge of my clit. It was maddening, and I kept repositioning myself to get her fingers to move up a smidgeon.

"Please stop teasing me," I called out between my rapid breaths.

"I really wish I'd brought my toys. You are so wet that it would slip right in and fill you up. Would you have liked that?" Serena asked.

"Oh, God, yes," I panted. "Can you go inside?"

She shifted our bodies again, so she was no longer propped on her side but continued to touch me from behind. The feel of her full body pressed tightly against me while fingering me from behind was all it took to cry out in ecstasy.

"Oh, fuck, that is so good."

I felt myself pulse against her fingers as she kept them deep inside me until the waves subsided. I wondered how much more fun we could have with her toys. I wanted Serena to fuck me until I couldn't move from the exhaustion of our lovemaking.

She didn't give me much time to recover as she flipped me onto my back, parted my legs, and buried her face in my dripping curls. I was glad I'd recently clipped my pubic hair because I didn't want her turned off by an unruly bush. I stopped having any other thoughts other than how fucking amazing her tongue felt on my clit. The tiny nibbles on the hood followed by her gentle sucking took me quickly over the edge not even five minutes after the previous mind-blowing orgasm. After the tremors stopped, she crawled up my body, looking quite pleased with herself.

Even though my legs and arms felt like rubber, I gathered a second wind and flipped her over. "My turn." I was eager to taste and touch every erogenous zone on her glorious body.

CHAPTER NINE

Melissa

Back to present day…

Walking into the bustling hospital, it felt good to have work to distract me. I visited Mary right away because she was the benefits specialist, and I needed to change my beneficiaries and health insurance.

I didn't know Mary well, but I liked her blunt, forthright manner, and she could be very funny sometimes. She told me about the single lesbian who ran the bakery in town.

"Um, thanks, but I'm not looking to date right now."

"Oh, hey, you should sign up for Match.com."

"Not you too. I just got strong-armed into that by my friends on the island."

"Ooh, we're all old married women, so you have to show us the profiles of anyone who winks at you."

I didn't want to admit I hadn't looked at the site yet, but I couldn't lie. "Um, I haven't gone into my profile to check."

"What? Why not? I'll bet you have a boatload of winks. You're actually attractive for a lesbian."

I raised my eyebrow at her, and I think she realized what she'd just said.

"Oh, sorry. I didn't mean it like that. I just mean you're really pretty."

"So, is that all I need to do to remove her?" I decided to change the subject.

"Yep, that's it. You're all set. Melissa, look at the site tonight, okay? It would be good to see you smile again, and I guarantee it will be good for your ego to check. Oh, hey, I forgot to ask you what you want to do with your cell phone plan."

I scrunched up my face and asked, "What do you mean?"

"Well, you don't want to keep Colette on the plan, do you?"

"Oh, yeah, I guess I forgot about that."

Then I thought that since I'd been paying the bills, I was entitled to see who she was calling. I knew this was likely to lead to further misery, but I couldn't help myself.

"Um, Mary, do you think I can get a complete accounting of who she's been calling, including the dates and times?"

"Oh, sure, I can call AT&T and get that for you."

"Okay, that would be great."

†

66

I walked out of Mary's office and didn't give my request a second thought. I headed to my office and began fixing my queries in the employee database.

Mary gave a quick knock and entered.

I had an open-door policy and interruptions never bothered me. "What can I help you with?"

She handed me a stack of papers, and I sent her a questioning look.

"It's the last two months of activity on your cell phone account."

"Oh, okay. Thanks for getting this so quickly."

Mary walked out of my office and left me to scour over the records.

Scanning the phone records, it all came crashing down. I realized Colette was on the phone with her lover while I was downstairs at six o'clock in the morning working on *her* PowerPoint presentation for her advanced respiratory care class. Of course, I didn't know squat about respiratory care, but I'm an expert researcher, and I knew what to pull from the internet to jazz up her presentation. I ended up spending hours on her class project while she probably had phone sex with her girlfriend.

Everything culminated into a perfect storm. All those years of being a doormat and telling my ex-girlfriend I will look the other way while she has her fling or asking if my other ex is sure she's in love with her bandmate. I realized I was paying for a cell phone my girlfriend was using to call her new soulmate in Alaska.

For the very first time in my life, I was furious, and I stopped thinking I deserved this for whatever screwy reason I always gave myself. I started thinking mean things like *I* hope *Karma will take care of Colette, and this new fling dumps her ass before she even moves completely out of my place.*

In the past, I had always stayed friends with my other exes, even making sure to take care of them financially and helping out when I could. This time, I didn't want to be her friend. I wanted her out of my life for good.

†

Marching into Mary's office, through gritted teeth, I directed, "Please cancel my second phone."

"You got it, boss. Um, I know it's none of my business, but Colette is a fool. You ought to check your Match.com account. I'll bet those single lesbians will be beating down your door."

My face instantly turned scarlet. I was not accustomed to talking with the people I worked with about personal things.

"I don't think it's my cup of tea," I quietly answered.

"Oh, you should, really you should. I say the best revenge is to find someone new that you can be happy with. You have to show us all your prospects so that we can assess them for you."

I shuffled out of the office, embarrassed that my personal life was flayed open for all to see. It would take another month before the loneliness and isolation got to me, and I decided to find a few more like-minded lesbians who I could do things with on the weekends. No strings or romantic entanglements attached.

CHAPTER TEN

Colette

I was on cloud nine. Serena had asked me to move to Alaska and live with her. I'd only ever worked on a fishing boat in Alaska, and I knew that was nothing like what she was offering. Although I wasn't sure what to do with the dogs, I could figure that out. I decided to call Candie. She was always very accommodating, and hopefully, she hadn't taken sides like everyone else.

Summer school was coming to a close, and I figured I needed to complete my commitment before deciding if it was possible to continue schooling in Alaska. Hospitals were always in need of respiratory therapists. I sat back in the chair of my rented room in the attic. I'd done everything I could to make the space mine, so it was comfortable. First order of business was to take care of Red and Blackie. I picked up my phone from my desk and made the call to Candie.

"Hello."

"Hey, Candie. It's Colette. I was wondering if you could take care of Red and Blackie. They're good dogs and are used to staying outside. They have that dog room they can go to whenever they want to get out of the weather."

"What does Melissa think of this idea?"

"Um… well, I haven't exactly asked her. She wants them gone from Cle Elum because she doesn't want the responsibility, so I figured this was a good option. You know them and like dogs, right?"

"Yeah… but… look, I don't want to get in the middle of your shit, and besides, my loyalty is to Melissa. She's letting me stay here for free. I owe her a ton."

"What if I clear it with Melissa? Would you be willing to take care of them if it was okay with her?"

"I suppose so."

"Great, I'll call her and clear it with her."

"Um… some advice?"

"Sure." I couldn't believe I agreed to listen to this youngster who was still struggling with her own sexuality and religious chains from her parents.

"Give her a little space. She's barely hanging on."

The pit landed heavily in my stomach. I was the cause of this beautiful person's sadness. How could I ever live with that? I was a selfish prig after all.

"I know." What else could I say?

†

Before class, I searched on the internet for a school in Anchorage and was delighted to learn that Charter College had a program. I hung back after the lecture to talk with one of my favorite instructors. I wanted to know how well my credits would transfer to another school. He seemed disappointed I wouldn't finish my final quarter, but he didn't have the answers for me because every school was different.

I pushed this hurdle from my mind and decided it wasn't all that important. I could always return to school. The most important thing was finding my way to where my soulmate lived. The rest would all work out. We had the ultimate connection.

I was wondering how I was going to approach Melissa when my cell phone rang. The pit returned when I saw it was Melissa.

"Hello."

"I'm sorry, but I thought you should know that I canceled your cell phone from my plan. You can keep the number, but you're on your own for the costs. Oh, and I called the credit card companies to remove you from the cards. Since we are no longer domestic partners, I had to remove you from my health insurance plan. You're only covered until the end of the month."

"Okay." *Shit.* The reality of the situation hit me hard. I needed to find a job in Alaska, quick. I decided I better get my favor out of the way since she seemed in control at the moment. "I talked to Candie, and she's willing to take care of the dogs if that's okay with you. I'll come get them this coming weekend."

"Fine. I'll be at a rainbow ride so you can pick them up on Saturday. That works out better anyway. I wasn't sure how I was going to fit the dogs and my bike in the car."

"Can I keep a key to the Cle Elum house so that I can come get my stuff when I have time?"

She hesitated before responding, "I suppose that makes sense. I already bought a new dresser, so yours is in the living room taking up space, ready for you to get it. There wasn't a lot to pack up."

"I know." I was saying that a lot, but this time, it was starting to sink in. That hit me hard. I realized that with me living in Seattle during the week, most of my belongings were already out of the house. It was like we'd already split over a year ago, and this was the final thread to sever.

The strand was like a spider's web, strong and yet so thin. I'd always managed to push the strand aside after realizing it was in the way. All the messy beauty of those silk strands woven into a pattern that never deviated. This was my pattern, falling out of love with genuinely nice women who loved and adored me until I felt strangled by that love. It only took three years with my previous ex; this time I'd survived eight. I was sure Serena was my forever woman, and there would be no more restlessness after the honeymoon wore off.

CHAPTER ELEVEN

Melissa

Now that I'd told Colette I wouldn't be there that weekend, I had to follow through. I hadn't wanted her to know what a pathetic loser I was with nothing at all to do on the weekends but wallow in my own misery. I'd made the impulsive call to tell her I'd cut her off financially. Before the call, I was waffling about whether to head to Issaquah for the end of the month ride in July. No more indecision. I had to commit now.

The universe is a total bitch sometimes as the songs playing on the radio somehow reminded me of Colette. I knew it was my mind playing tricks, looking for connections, but after several painful sing-a-longs, I decided quiet reflection was a better choice. It wasn't.

Mercifully, I reached the riding start point. I was the first one to arrive and busied myself with pumping up my bike tires, lubing my chain, and attaching my bags with the treats I'd bought at a Safeway I found on the way to the ride.

I was mentally preparing myself for the looks of pity on my friend's faces when Nadine, the leader of the Rainbow Riders, approached. She didn't say a word as she gathered me into a hug.

Fuck a duck. I was crying again. That's all it took. There wasn't anything I hated more than crying in front of other people. I always saved that for when I was completely alone.

"Please don't make me talk about it. I just want to get lost in the ride and enjoy our monthly time together." I groaned. "Shit, I sound like we're all having our period at the same time. You know what I mean."

She nodded. "You know there are a lot of riders who ride on the off weekends. You can connect with them. Veronica is always looking for someone to bike with, and she lives on the island."

"Good idea. She'll be here today, right?"

"Yeah, she rarely misses a rainbow ride."

I felt my face scrunch up. "She's kind of an animal, though. I'll probably puke after the first hill she'll lead me up. I'm not sure I can keep up with her."

Nadine waved her hand in the air. "Are you kidding? I'm the one that brings it up the rear." She laughed. "Now, I've said something that sounds, you know, far worse than your monthly comment. Anyway, my point is, you are always in front of the pack, and I lag behind with the more leisurely riders."

That generated a chuckle from me. Yes, I tended to hang with the leaders, but that was only because my competitive side came out. It was damn hard to keep up with Veronica, especially since my recumbent bike was considerably slower on hills. I could climb them, but not nearly as fast as an upright, or rather an up-*wrong* bike, as I named the racers. Hers was a light, sleek machine while mine was for pure pleasure and exercise.

"I've not been riding as much lately, so I might be a bit out of shape," I confessed. Curling up in a ball every night after work, after apologizing to your beloved bike for not taking her out again, does that to a person.

Nadine glanced up and down my body. "Don't lose any more weight. You're about to blow away already."

"I know. Food hasn't been appetizing lately."

"How much weight have you lost?"

"Only ten pounds or so."

"Yeah, well, that was ten pounds you couldn't afford to lose. You were already an itty-bitty thing."

"Alcohol has a lot of calories. Maybe I should drink more," I joked.

"Not funny."

I sent thanks to the universe when the rest of the group pulled into the parking lot and effectively cut short our conversation. I didn't need a reminder of what I already knew. Destructive behavior in the form of not eating was not healthy. I'd have to talk a bit more about that with my therapist.

†

The group was going out to eat after the ride, but I declined their invitation. It was a long trip back to Cle Elum. I had decided not to drive to Whidbey because I didn't want to take the chance I would run into Colette. With my luck, she'd be dropping off Red and Blackie at the same time I rolled into the driveway of my house on the island.

I was exhausted from the ride, and when I returned home, I grabbed my bike and rolled it into the makeshift garage in the basement of the chalet. We'd laid plastic down in the bedroom and turned the room into a storage shed.

Big Red, our tandem recumbent bike, glared at me. *I should sell that monstrosity.* Single meant the two-person bike was about as useful as leathers without a motorcycle. That reminded me of the top of the line helmet sitting on the shelf in the closet. I needed it for when I was a passenger on Colette's 650cc bike.

Colette had received a windfall when her mother died, and she'd used most of it on a motorcycle and all the gear a person could think of to spruce it up. She was generous enough to purchase the gear for me. It was a thoughtful gift and expensive. This time, I hadn't paid for it or paid off a loan for her dream truck. I'd only co-signed for it and helped a little here and there.

I tossed my bike bag into the room and shut the door. Out of sight, out of mind.

I didn't quite know what to do with myself. I didn't have any homework to help Colette with or website projects. I was at a loss. I had a lot of free time, and it was rather unsettling.

Alone in my chalet and throwing myself a huge pity party, I resumed my nightly cryfest. In an act of desperation, I stomped down to my office and turned on my computer to see if Veronica was interested in getting together for a bike ride or something the following weekend. I knew I couldn't go to the island on all my days off and depend on my friends to entertain me while I overcame my heartbreak.

†

I went to the Match.com site and relished putting in my password—*Colettesabitch*. There was something very cathartic about typing that in. *Thank you, Tori.*

I was amazed to see twenty winks, and I quickly scrolled through the messages. Two stood out.

One was an extremely attractive woman who was some kind of competitive swimmer. I don't swim at all, and we had nothing in common, but she was hot, so I sent back a quick reply. Remember, I wasn't looking for a wife, but hanging out with an attractive lesbian sounded appealing.

The other looked like a granola type lesbian, but I couldn't tell because she was sporting sunglasses in the picture. What pulled me in was her words.

I must say that I was attracted to you and your words. I've been sitting on my account for 1.5 years. The only thing is I'm batting 2/2. One is that I'm a year older from your cut off age, and I'm within 75 miles instead of 50. However, I do travel to the Yakima area for business from time to time. Perhaps if you come to this side of the mountains and go to the San Juan Islands, we could forego the 50 miles. I'm not sure what to say, as I am truly a puppy at this. Peace, Christine.

She sucked me in. For some reason, I wanted to know more about this person, so I gave myself a little pep talk. I was smacking myself on the head because I wasn't sure why I let Tori put in an age range. There were women in my bike group over sixty who still kept up with the lead group. *Okay, remember, you only want more lesbian friends who are single and can simply hang out.*

All my friends on the island were couples, except Candie, so I didn't want to continue to be the fifth wheel.

I sent back a message.

I joined Match on the encouragement of some dear friends. I am recently single and, honestly, still healing from that, so at this point, I am only reaching out to develop some new friendships, not yet ready for dating.

There, I'd laid out the ground rules, now I had to correct Tori's well-intentioned response on the age range.

Since I am now 45, 51 seems young. I honestly don't know why there is an age range in the profile because as long as someone is active, age makes no difference, especially in friendships.

Before I had a chance to edit my reply, I pushed the send button. I groaned as my lame response blinked back at me.

And so began our month-long correspondence.

CHAPTER TWELVE

Colette

I still had a small amount of money from my inheritance. So, on a whim, I got on my laptop and looked for tickets to Alaska. I was going to surprise Serena. Yesterday, she'd gone back home after her visit with her mom. I already missed her.

Serena was beginning to express her concern about how fast things were moving, and she didn't want to be the cause of me not finishing school. She didn't want me to regret making such a big life change. I played the conversation over in my head looking for clues. I wanted to believe she was only concerned about what was best for me, and subsequently us, as we planned our future. Three months wasn't a long time to wait, but it might as well have been three years because I already missed her.

She'd been making lazy circles on my stomach as we lay on the bed in her cottage after making love.

"You know," she began, "three months is a very short amount of time. I think you should finish school first. We can talk every night." The last part felt like a bone tossed out to make me feel better.

I turned my head to catch her eyes, and it seemed like she was avoiding direct eye contact. "I know my friends Tori and Janet lived apart for two years while Janet was working in San Diego, but I'm not wired like them."

"They're still going strong, right?"

"Yeah, they are, but they're special. This is the second time they've endured living apart. The way they look at each other, there isn't another person who could ever get in the middle of their love." And there it was. My insecurities were already getting in the way. I thought if I didn't move there with her, right this second, she would find someone new. She was my soulmate, but was I hers? How did that exactly work?

"We're special too. Musically, we're magic together."

"Musically? Is that all?"

"Of course not. The sex is mind-blowing."

"I told Melissa you were more than a good time in bed. I'm not leaving an eight-year relationship for someone that's good in the sac and that I harmonize well with. We connect. I believe in soulmates now. I never did before."

"I'm not good at expressing myself in words. I don't know if such a thing as soulmates exists, but our chemistry is undeniable. I get you, and you get me. We're both musicians and can express our feelings through music. I knew the first time I heard your CD that we were meant to connect."

Serena jumped from the bed and grabbed her guitar. "I wrote a song for you. I want you to listen."

The world tilted back on its axis. She wrote me a song. That was as good as those three little words *I love you*, which I hadn't quite heard yet.

†

We'd agreed to take time to consider whether a move now or a move later was better. Since I had a couple of weeks off between quarters, I thought it was the perfect time to visit. I was so excited when I called Serena that I let my enthusiasm overpower the conversation.

"Hey, I'm glad you called. I was missing you."

That was the perfect greeting. "Would you like a visitor?"

"A visitor?"

"Yeah. I know we are still evaluating the timing of the move, but I got to thinking how there wasn't anything stopping me from visiting while on break."

"Sure, that'd be great, but I have to work during the day. I recently took several weeks off so I won't be able to spend a lot of time with you."

"We'll have the evenings, right?"

"We will."

She sounded hesitant.

"You don't seem pleased."

"Oh no, it's not that. It's just that I wish I had time to show you around. Alaska is exceptionally beautiful, and it's better if you have a proper tour guide."

81

"I know it is, I've been to Ketchikan, but never Anchorage. I'm excited about the trip. I can figure out a way to your place or hang at the airport as long as you need me to if you can't come get me because of work or something."

"Okay."

I was expecting her to protest and say she would be there and figure out work, but I suppose having recently returned from vacation, it wasn't an option. I convinced myself it wasn't a big deal.

"I'll send you the details in an e-mail. I'll see you in two days," I enthused.

"Okay, thanks. Hey listen, I gotta go. I promised Noya I would sit in with her on a set tonight. You'll love Noya. She's an incredible musician, as good as you. She has a large following here, so it's a huge thing that she asked me to sit in with her. You understand, right?"

"Uh huh."

"Talk to you later, Colette."

Dead air. I set my phone down on the desk and wondered if I was making—or had made a huge mistake.

†

Washington was a beautiful state with the mountains and sound, and I knew Alaska had a similar type of splendor, but to see the view from the airplane was nothing short of awe-inspiring. I thought the words in the song "America the Beautiful" about the mountains aptly described what I was seeing—even though Alaska hadn't become a state until sixty-six years after Katharine Lee Bates had written the song.

My legs jiggled up and down in excitement. Serena wasn't able to pick me up, but the airport wasn't far from her studio apartment, so I splurged on a cab ride to her place and then found my way to the bar after dropping my bags off. She'd apologized profusely, but Noya had asked her to sit in again for a set, and she couldn't pass up the opportunity. She was giddy with the thrill of her future prospects, and I shared her enthusiasm. I knew what it felt like for someone you admired to ask you to sit in. This was often the first step to joining a band—the typical manner in which musicians conducted interviews. I wondered where I might fit in since we'd talked about forming our own band.

I knew Serena had a small place, but I hadn't realized it was an apartment building. The modern brick structure was not at all what I had expected. I thought maybe she lived in an artsy neighborhood like Freemont or Wallingford. Even though I didn't live in either of those suburbs, I thought the fit was better than where I currently rented a room.

I pulled out the handle to my large bag and then rolled it up the sidewalk and into the lobby where I could catch the elevator to the fourth floor. Waiting patiently at 405 where her neighbor lived, I felt a little lost.

A tall, thin man with a shaved head opened the door a crack and peered out at me. "You Colette?"

I nodded. "Gary?"

He thrust a key at me, and once the key was in my hand, he shut the door.

"Ah, the friendly sort," I mumbled.

Since I was eager to see Serena, I set my bag inside the door after unlocking it. I didn't even take the time to look around her place. The place was small, that much was evident, and I noted the lack of room for two large dogs. Tossing away any concerns, like unwanted garbage, I decided there was plenty of time to look for a new place with a fenced backyard.

The yellow cab idled in front of the apartment building because I'd asked him to wait a few minutes. He shrugged and mumbled his agreement. I watched him toss his cigarette on the ground and smash it with his foot. I didn't like leaving the butt on the sidewalk, but I wasn't going to pick it up with my bare hands.

†

A thick cloud of smoke invaded my nostrils as soon as I entered the bar. The prohibition against smoking in public places did not take effect until 2007 in Anchorage. It was particularly harsh for musicians who often made their living in the small, crowded bars where everyone lit up. Whenever our band played, by the end of the evening, my throat was raw from the combination of singing for three hours and smoke inhalation.

Serena was facing an attractive woman, strumming on her guitar, and harmonizing to "Big Yellow Taxi" by Joni Mitchell. They sounded good. Our small band had often played that song. It was a crowd favorite. After the song finished, she bent her head and whispered something in the woman's ear. They looked awfully cozy. I felt my dream start to slip.

My wave was anemic, but apparently, I was hard to miss as I walked in front of the small stage. Serena nodded and then they started a new song.

During the break, Serena and the singer walked over to the table where I sat by myself patiently waiting for the small band to finish.

"You made it. Colette, this is Noya. Isn't she incredible?" Serena enthused.

I shook the hand extended to me. "Hi. Nice set."

"Serena said you're a musician too. Maybe you can join in on a song."

"I didn't bring my guitar."

"I have an extra," Noya offered.

I felt the tug to meld with other musicians and try to prove I could hold my own with this person who Serena seemed enamored with. "All right, I'd love to."

"Great. Let me get the set list, and you can tell me if you think there are any songs you would like to join in on." She walked back to the stage and picked up several sheets of paper tucked under one of the effects pedals.

When she handed me the list, I looked at the scribbles on the paper and picked out "Angel from Montgomery" by Bonnie Raitt and John Prine. Our small band always sang that song because it was one of Lanie's favorites. I pointed to the song nearly at the bottom of the list. "This would be a good song to join in on, I know it well."

"Cool. I'll motion for you to come up right before we sing that one. You can take the mic that Serena is on, and my other guitar is the Guild next to my Martin over there." She pointed to a beautiful instrument with what looked like a spruce top and solid mahogany back. I was sure this guitar would have a powerful, full crisp sound.

When I looked up at Serena, I was smiling, but she was frowning. I didn't want to muscle in on her gig, but Noya had asked. "Serena, are you okay with me sitting in for a song?"

A smile returned to Serena's face, but it looked forced. "Of course, it'll be great to have your added talents."

†

It was late when we returned to Serena's apartment. She was quiet on the way home.

"Is something wrong?" I asked.

Tossing her bag on the chair and setting her guitar case down, she answered, "No, I'm just tired and have to get up early for work. I didn't have time to stock the fridge, but there's a store not too far from here."

Grabbing my bag, I followed her into the bedroom. She started shedding her clothes until she was in her underwear and then she pulled open a drawer and grabbed a T-shirt. Standing in her bedroom still holding onto my bag, I felt a little lost. "I can get some food and cook for us tomorrow. I'll have dinner ready for when you come home. What time?"

"Around six," she grunted and then disappeared into the tiny bathroom. I heard her brushing her teeth.

My enormous rolling suitcase signaled my hope for a long, full visit. I'd packed enough for two weeks, the time I'd planned to stay. I wasn't sure if there was room for me to put away my clothes, or if she wanted me to grab from my case. Since she hadn't offered an empty drawer, I carefully set the bag down and unzipped it. Pawing through my luggage, it took me a few minutes to find my own T-shirt for sleeping in. Serena had definitely signaled she wasn't up for anything but sleeping tonight. I had hoped to make love, but that clearly was not on the itinerary.

I pushed aside some of my clothes and found my bath bag. Passing her, I brushed my teeth in silence. When I returned to the bedroom, Serena was already under the covers. When she said goodnight, she hadn't kissed me. In fact, she hadn't kissed me when I arrived. Something was definitely amiss.

When she rolled to her side away from me, I snuggled up against her and draped my arm across her stomach. "Goodnight, honey," I whispered in her ear. She was probably exhausted after working all day and then playing the gig tonight, I rationalized.

CHAPTER THIRTEEN

Melissa

Rushing home from work, I jogged down the stairs to boot up my computer. I'd sent a test balloon to Christine about joining the Rainbow Riders, my bike group, and found myself anxious to hear her response. I'd been communicating back and forth with a few other cyclists and had invited them to the ride on the weekend, but Christine was the one I hoped would make it.

When I read her message, I did a mental high five.

I would definitely be interested in the information on the ride this coming weekend. I'm on call pretty much 24/7 but would love to try and get out to bike with a group of ladies. I moved out here with my partner in 96 from Maryland to go to Bastyr, only for her to leave in 97. It was a very painful breakup. I guess you can say I am more than cautious about getting to know other women of like minds. But here I am…plugging away. The Match.com seems so unnatural to me. However, if I come out with some good friends and a way to meet healthy women, then it was all worth the risk.

She asked for my phone number in case she needed to call. I wasn't good on the phone. I never had been, but I gave her my number. She called later that evening. I stuttered through the call.

Whenever I was nervous, I stuttered. I'd had to work very hard on that in high school and college. When my mother learned from my older sister that the theater teacher had mocked me, I thought she was going to rip the teacher a new asshole. After finishing basketball practice one day, I had arrived late to the theater. My nerves kicked in when trying to explain. That day I quit theater and never returned. Mom wanted to know why, and my sister quickly offered the answer.

I looked at the 206 area code, took a deep breath, and answered the phone.

"Hello."

"Hi, it's Christine. Is it okay that I called this late?"

"Sure. Th…th…that's fine." Crap, I was already stuttering.

"I'm nervous to meet you and your group."

I relaxed a little and spoke my words slowly, remembering what my therapist had taught me. "Don't be. Everyone in the group is super welcoming, and I'm a very down-to-earth person. I don't have any pre-conceived notions of anything, nor any expectations. Our group tends to ride, rain or shine. I know that sounds hardcore, but we aren't, and no one ever gets left behind."

"That sounds good because it's been a while since I rode. How is work going for you this week?"

I chuckled. "Tomorrow, I agreed to be in the hospital's dunk tank. Employees love to dunk administrators. I searched for the perfect outfit at the Goodwill, the ugliest formal-wear gown I could find. I did have this dream last night that I forgot my swimsuit, which I intend to wear under the dress. Anyway, in my dream, I wasn't wearing any undergarments, and when I was dunked, the whole world saw a bit more than intended."

Christine laughed, and that settled me even more. "That's a new twist to the naked-in-a-public-place dream that a lot of people have. Trust me, right about now, I feel as vulnerable as your latest dream seems to indicate."

"Vulnerable. That's a good word for how I'm feeling."

"We can be vulnerable together."

"D…d…deal." My stuttering was back.

"I think you're brave for putting yourself out there and trying to meet new people. I better let you get to sleep. Good night, Melissa. I'll see you in a few days."

"Thanks for calling. Good night, Christine."

I set the phone on my nightstand and scooted down under the covers with my furbabies cuddled next to me. I thought about the upcoming ride as I stroked their fur, one hand on each cat.

†

I needed fresh air, exercise, and a new perspective on life or I was destined to lock myself away for the rest of my pitiful days on earth. My good friends on the island were doing everything in their power to keep me from making any self-destructive choices. I felt proud of myself for taking this first step to get out and socialize.

I'd been communicating with another woman regularly. I wasn't sure why I agreed to have coffee with the woman my staff nicknamed "Swimmer Girl." I'd made the mistake of caving to their constant prods to show me pictures of anyone who had winked at me, and they'd decided Swimmer Girl was a perfect match. I kept reminding them I wasn't looking for a new girlfriend. They weren't listening.

The weekend was fast approaching, and I'd decided after my rainbow ride, I would connect with my island friends, crash at their house again, and then, on my way back to Cle Elum, I would meet Swimmer Girl for coffee. I had my whole weekend planned, so I didn't have to return to a forty-eight-hour cryfest sequestered in my little chalet.

As I lay in bed, I experienced my first night without tears. I was starting to heal.

CHAPTER FOURTEEN

Sarasota

My human was scratching my fur, just the way I liked. Something was different about her tonight. I didn't mind it when the water came out of her eyes and got on my fur. It wasn't like when she tried to give me a bath. Besides, I knew she needed my brother and me.

"I like this woman, Sarasota. What the hell am I thinking? I don't need another damn heartbreak. It's only been a couple of months."

"Meow," I reassured her.

"Meow," Freud chimed in.

I stood up and smacked Freud on the head with one of my paws. "Meow. Bwrup." I told Freud to hush because what did he know. He's a boy, they don't experience heartache like girls.

"Sarasota, why'd you do that?"

92

"Meow." Freud jumped off the bed in a huff. I think he was irritated with both of us.

Melissa chuckled. It was good to hear her laugh again. "You are a jealous little thing. I suppose it's just us girls now. You shouldn't treat your brother that way. You know how sensitive he is."

Sensitive, my ass. Freud was a big baby who liked to hog all the attention. I turned around in circles and settled on her chest. It was just us girls, the way I liked it. It was rare that I had Melissa's attention all to myself. Freud always had to worm his way in and would tuck up into her arms when she slept on her side, resting his head on her shoulder. I had to find another place since he snagged the coveted spot. But tonight, it was all about me. I purred loudly. Freud might secure the cherry place in the bed, but Melissa always talked to me.

"I think I'm in trouble, Sarasota. There's something about Christine that I'm drawn to. She has this energy about her. I suppose it's a plus that she's fifty-one. Maybe an older woman will be better for me. I gotta break the mold somehow. From now on, my new motto is an artist-free zone. And no more women younger than me. They never seem to be settled enough not to trade me in for a younger model."

I didn't answer because I knew she was trying to work it all out on her own. She didn't need any advice from me. I was the one who had made friends with Colette first. I didn't want her remembering that and thinking poorly of me. Yup, purring was the only safe option.

CHAPTER FIFTEEN

Colette

The first couple of days in Alaska were awkward. I found the store around the corner, and because I had plenty of time, I prepared a feast for her that first full day. Her appreciation was genuine, but I still felt like something was missing.

Serena put her hand over the wine glass when I went to fill it up again. "No more for me. I don't drink on the weekdays. Maybe you should slow down too."

I set the wine on the table without refilling my glass for the third time. I didn't want to start an argument, but Serena was beginning to sound like Melissa.

"You don't work on the weekends, do you?" I asked.

"Sometimes they call me in when there is a big sale pending. I help my boss put together the paperwork, and they pay overtime for that."

"Oh. I suppose we can't make any definite plans then."

"I tried to tell you I probably wouldn't have a lot of time, but I'm glad you could visit. We'll find time for me to show you around. At least you came in the summer. It's the best time to visit."

"That's okay, I'll take whatever free time you have."

"Listen, Noya did invite me to go kayaking with her on Saturday if I don't work. Maybe we can rustle up a double or another kayak."

I wanted to spend some alone time with Serena, but I answered how I was expected to. "That sounds like fun." Mom had always drilled politeness into me, almost to the point of dishonesty. It was a hard habit to break.

†

After Serena came home from work at the real estate office on Friday, it felt like we might get on track. She'd pulled me in her arms and swung me around. She was in a good mood because Noya had called to invite her to sit in again on another gig.

I'd set the table, lit some candles, and created yet another gourmet dinner for the two of us. She waved away the wine because she said she needed to be sober to play well. I was on my second glass. I'd already decided I wasn't going to hone in on her gig because I got the sense she wasn't pleased when I joined them for that one song. "Listen, I don't want to interject myself into the symmetry you and Noya have going, so maybe you could talk to her and let her know I just want to listen tonight." I wanted her to shine, not have me hog the stage.

Serena beamed at me. "Thanks. She's off on tour in a few weeks, so I wanted to take advantage of the time we have, and maybe she'll consider me for her band in the future. I heard she's not getting along with her partner, and they might break up. That's why I've been sitting in. She's in Florida right now visiting with her mom who's really sick, I guess."

"That can be a tough time for someone. It was for Melissa and me when my mom was dying."

"Yeah, I suppose, but she should understand that Noya can't cancel all her gigs to be by her side."

Warning bells were going off again, so I shifted to a related subject. "When I move up here, we can form our own band. We just need a drummer."

"We could," she hedged, "but getting into an established band is so much easier. We'll see how it all pans out. Things always work out the way they're supposed to. No sense in making any life-changing decisions yet. If she asks me to tour with her, that'll mean quitting my job and going on the road. You probably wouldn't want to travel as a groupie, especially since you're a talented musician in your own right. Too bad you don't have the kind of following Noya has."

Noya, Noya, Noya. It's always about Noya. That name was starting to crawl up my ass and not in a good way. "The music business is very competitive," I mumbled.

Serena pushed away from the table. "That was scrumptious, but I gotta get in the shower before I head to the bar tonight. Sorry to leave you with the mess, but I'm running late."

"That's okay. I'll clean up while you get ready."

†

Jealousy. That's what I felt as I watched Noya and Serena sing together. Noya was good, that much I'll give her, but she wasn't even trying to hide her flirtations. Serena was eating it up.

I hadn't told Serena that I'd already started to pack up my place and begin the arrangements to move to Alaska. Part of the reason I'd decided to visit was to look for work.

During the day, I began looking for a job as a cook. I wanted to surprise her with how easy it would be to make the move. Lining up employment was the most important piece to have in place. I didn't want to feel like I had with Melissa. I'd barely contributed financially to the relationship, and that was a big part of the problem. I didn't like feeling chained to her out of practicality. Once I obtained gainful employment, then I was sure the rest would fall together quickly. It was just a matter of finishing packing my limited belongings and tossing them in the truck.

My truck was important to me, and I didn't want to sell it, so I was hoping Serena would take more time off work, fly back to Washington, and drive the truck back to Alaska with me. We could make it an adventure. I knew that driving all the way to Alaska by myself wasn't remotely a good idea.

Serena nearly bounced over to the table I was sitting at. I was on my fourth glass of wine. "Hey, how do we sound?"

I plastered a smile on my face. "Incredible."

"Yeah, I feel like we're nailing it tonight. Thanks for coming."

Where else would I go? I must have looked at her cross-eyed.

"Oh, I mean, thanks for being a good sport and tagging along. I know this wasn't exactly what you had in mind when you planned your visit."

"No, no, it's great. I always love listening to good music, and it's a bonus that you're on stage to listen to," I assured her.

She leaned down and pecked me on the lips. "You're the best. Hey, by the way, I've been trying to learn this complicated riff, and I was wondering if you would help me out with that on Sunday? Noya wanted me to learn it, ya know, just in case."

Dread hit my stomach, twisting my intestines like a pretzel.

†

None of my misgivings stayed, because that night, Serena attacked my body like our lovemaking on the first night. After the gig, she was hyped up, and we barely made it inside her small apartment. She'd dragged me to the bedroom and pulled my clothes off like they were on fire and she needed to remove them lest they burn my skin.

The desperation in her craving to be skin on skin paced my own. "I need you under me, now," she directed.

We giggled as she tossed me on the bed and playfully grabbed the edge of my bikini briefs with her teeth. I could feel her teeth scrape across the top of my closely cropped mound as she tugged hard to remove the barrier. I lifted my ass to make it easier.

Both of her large hands massaged each thigh as she made her way up my body and then cupped my behind. I spread my legs in anticipation of her tongue.

The first long stroke sent shivers up my back. She used the flat surface and then latched on to my clit, sucking gently at first.

"Harder, suck harder," I ordered.

She obliged, and then I felt two fingers plunge inside. My vagina didn't offer any resistance as a generous amount of lubrication allowed her to slip in and out.

I was bucking wildly now as the feeling of approaching the edge swelled until I was so close, I begged her to let me come. "Please, don't stop. I'm so close."

Her fingers reached deep, all the way inside to my cervix. I'd heard of cervical orgasms before but never experienced them. This was what an all-body orgasm felt like. My release exploded, and I felt the tingles all the way from my head to my toes.

"Holy shit," I exclaimed as the feeling continued for several minutes.

Serena slid up my body and rocked her clit against my leg. "That was so hot. I'm so close after watching and feeling you." She arched her back and called out as she lifted and came a few seconds later. "Oh, wow, that was incredible."

She flipped on her back and tried to slow her breathing. I curled next to her, needing the closeness after our powerful explosion of pleasure. "Tell me that we won't ever lose this. I can't go back to lesbian bed-death again."

Chuckling, Serena answered, "I like sex too much, but God it does seem to infect lesbians more than straights. I don't really understand why."

"I read something somewhere that clarified that although lesbians have sex more infrequently when in long-term relationships, the quality is superior."

"Quality?" She turned and smiled.

"Yes, apparently, we have sex for longer than thirty minutes and often for hours."

"Oh right. Well, after I catch my breath, we might as well make sure we live up to that standard."

We made love three more times, and I was happy when Noya called the next morning to cancel the kayaking adventure. I needed to fill my tank back up because I was dangerously close to empty.

CHAPTER SIXTEEN

Melissa

As our correspondence and phone calls continued, I learned Christine was a research scientist at Children's Hospital in Seattle. She was kind and thoughtful, and I was looking forward to meeting her in person at the upcoming Rainbow Riders bike ride. I didn't give it much thought when I'd invited several other women who I was communicating with whom shared my passion for cycling. I intended to gain new friendships with individuals I could spend time with that would take me out of the house, not obtain a new girlfriend. But fate had a different plan for me.

The day of the ride came, and I was so nervous to meet Christine. I arrived a half hour early to center myself.

The rest of the group slowly trickled in as we converged on the pre-arranged meeting site.

The ride leaders, Nadine and Sammie, startled me when they knocked on my window.

I took a deep breath as I stepped out and received extended hugs from both of them. I'm sure they could see how emotionally fragile I was.

"Melissa, how are you really doing?" Nadine asked.

I choked back my tears and told her, "I'm fine." I immediately changed the subject. "I hope it's okay. I invited someone new."

"Of course it is. You know we love to fold new people into our group." Nadine shifted her gaze to the left and pointed at the Isuzu that had just pulled up. "Is that her?"

I squinted in the early morning sunshine. "I don't know. I haven't met her in person."

Nadine's eyebrow raised. "Okay, well, you might want to see if it's her or not."

A beautiful woman with a stylish haircut and a dazzling smile stepped out of the car with a bundle of what looked like freshly cut lavender in her hands.

She walked over. "Melissa?"

I nodded and felt the flush rise to my face. She looked vaguely like her picture, but with the different haircut, she was like a completely different person. Her smile mesmerized me.

"Christine?"

She nodded then handed me the lavender. "They have healing properties. I thought you might want them."

This time, the flush went all the way to my toes. A pretty smile always did that to me.

I mumbled a quick thank you and placed the offering in my car. The next thing I did may seem odd, but it made perfect sense to me. I glanced at her footwear and nodded appreciatively. *Check.* That was at least one thing on my list, and no, I didn't have a shoe fetish. With the help of my friends and not less than three Mike's Hard Lemonades, I developed a list of must haves for my next girlfriend. On the top of that list was *must have a passion for cycling.* How did I know in a glance she had a passion for cycling or was at least a serious cyclist? I noted that she wore biking shoes specifically designed for lock-in peddles.

I glanced up at her bike attached to the top of her vehicle and confirmed that, yes indeed, her bike had the clipless peddles. The special peddles had been around for quite some time. They were an enhancement to the old ones with metal clips you had to slip in and out of after tugging or loosening the strap to allow for your foot to safely disengage from the clip. It was an innovation that cyclists had stolen from skiers to enhance their efficiency by nearly twenty percent.

I shook my head and came out of my internal monologue of praise for the correct footwear and offered, "Do you need help to get your bike down?"

She smiled at me. "Sure."

We got her bike down and pumped up her tires. I always brought my floor pump because I liked my tires fully pumped. It provided a better, faster ride.

Nadine, our ride leader, motioned for everyone to gather around, and we did our normal introductions and rules for the ride. Everyone must wear a helmet. If you're passing someone, you have to let them know. No one gets left behind. Go at your own pace because we'll stop often to have snacks and take in the scenery.

I loved the Rainbow Riders. We often joked it wasn't miles per hour, but hours per mile on our rides. We stopped so often to snack and talk that it felt more like a social affair than exercise. Food was always involved. In fact, sometimes I got up early on Rainbow Rider days and did my usual workout to ensure I acquired enough exercise for the day.

"Okay, peddle up gals," Nadine called out.

†

We all headed down the paved trail, and normally, I stayed on pace with the faster riders, but not today. I thought it was only good manners to hang back and ride with Christine since I'd invited her and she didn't know anyone in the group yet.

Christine wasn't exactly a slug, but I could tell it had been some time since she'd ridden twenty-five or more miles, even at the Rainbow Riders' pace which was not even ten miles an hour.

As we dodged other riders, rollerbladers, strollers, and joggers on the Centennial Trail on our way to the velodrome at Marymoor Park, I tried hard to hold an intelligent conversation and learn about Christine's research. She was wicked smart, but there was a reason I worked in the administrative side of hospitals. Christine managed E.Coli studies at Children's hospital, which meant she dealt in poop samples. Yes, she collected shit. She gave away coffee cards to nurses who would save bloody feces samples for her. Bloody diarrhea meant a possible case of E.Coli 0157, which was a deadly bacteria in children causing renal failure if the medical professionals did not recognize it early enough.

Christine was a crusader for children, but talking about bodily fluids was a bit disconcerting. I could tell she was brilliant and passionate. I focused on the passion and glossed over the clinical details. That was the reason I rarely ate lunch with nurses. That's all they ever seemed to talk about, and it grossed me out. The cavalier discussions about various fluids that oozed from the human body was more than I could handle.

When we finally arrived at the velodrome, Christine cemented her place of honor with the Rainbow Riders as she pulled from her bag various specialty cheeses and fruit. They oohed and aahed over the treats she had brought.

"I didn't know what to bring, so I went shopping at Whole Foods for some snacks to share." Christine unloaded cloth napkins, nuts, cheeses, apples, grapes, and a checkered blue cloth she laid out on the steel bench.

I laughed deeply, probably for the first time since Colette had dumped me.

"Oh, you're going to fit right in. This group loves their snack-time. That's a pretty fancy spread you've got going there," Nadine exclaimed.

The vultures hovered over her, and before we climbed back on our bikes for the second half of the ride, they'd devoured every morsel. She'd solidified her position in our rider hierarchy as the woman who brought the best snacks.

†

After the ride, I had plans to meet Tori and Janet for dinner in Seattle. I extended a last-minute invitation to Christine, but she had to work that night. I subconsciously checked item number two on my list of must haves in a partner. On the outside, I was still insisting I was not looking for a new girlfriend, but Christine was hitting every item on my list, and I couldn't help noticing.

Christine not only had one full-time job as a research coordinator, but she also took additional shifts for the security department. In fact, she was one of the hardest working individuals I had come to know.

We were hanging out in front of her car after securing both bikes. My Rainbow Rider pals were snickering off to the side, but I didn't care. I was delaying my departure until the very last moment. Finally, she had to leave, or she'd be late for work.

"I'll call you later," she said as she closed her car door.

"Okay." I could feel myself smile.

After Christine rolled away, I heard Nadine's bike cleats clip-clop on the blacktop as she approached while I was tossing my helmet and a bag of gear into the front seat. "She seems nice and fits well in our group." Nadine paused, and I could tell by her expression she wasn't quite sure how to say the next thing. "Be careful, Melissa. You just ended a long-term relationship, and it's easy to soothe your pain with a new love."

I felt the tears re-emerge in the corner of my eyes. "I didn't end my relationship. Colette did. And for the record, I'm not looking to set up house with anyone right now, no matter how gorgeous their smile is."

Nadine shook her head. "Uh huh." She patted me on the shoulder. "We're here for you. Don't forget you have a lot of friends who care."

I didn't want to cry again. I was much better at stuffing my emotions. So I nodded and closed the door to escape her penetrating gaze, effectively shutting off any further conversation.

†

I was in my car humming to a *Fifth Dimension* CD, and my phone made a noise. Normally, I didn't answer the phone while I was driving, but a quick glance told me it was Christine. She texted that she had a fun day biking with the group. I wasn't adept at text messages yet. What could it hurt to call her back and place the phone against my ear while continuing to drive with my left hand? I fumbled with the phone selecting the speed dial option while continuing to look up at the road. Christine's voice floated out of the tiny speaker.

"Hey. You didn't have to call back. Are you driving now?" she asked.

"Yeah, but it's okay, I can use my left hand to steer." I wasn't sure what possessed me to do this, but the words were out of my mouth before I could censor them. "Um, I was wondering… Oh, never mind."

"No, what? This sounds intriguing."

"Every year, I make the trek to Victoria, BC, with my best friends, Tori and Janet. Since your house is on the way to the island, maybe we could meet up for dinner or something? I'm heading there on Wednesday before the long weekend. We try to beat all the boat traffic and snag the best slips in the marina. They're very accommodating, and if we arrive too late, we end up tied up to other boats instead of in our own slip." I was rambling. I knew that, but I was a little nervous asking about dinner.

"I'd love to." Her response slid in between my rambling as I took a second to pause.

"Okay, um, what time? I figure I could be in Arlington by six. If you know of a good sushi restaurant, maybe we could imbibe in our mutual admiration of that ethnic delight." I groaned inside. *Ethnic delight?* Where the hell did that come from?

"I know the perfect place, it's not my favorite spot, but it will do in a pinch. Six is perfect."

"Great. It's a date. Um, I mean… not a date, but—"

"I know what you meant." She chuckled, and the tension seemed to dissipate just a smidgeon. "You better concentrate on driving now. I sense a bit of fluster, and that is a recipe for disaster. I'll talk to you later. Have fun with your friends."

"Thanks, Christine. Have a good night. Sorry you have to work. Bye."

I wasn't sure if I was happy it wasn't a true date or not, but too late for that now. She seemed to know I needed a little space. After all, it had only been two months since Colette dumped me. It was way too soon for a real date. Friends. We could be friends, right?

CHAPTER SEVENTEEN

Colette

Serena's phone rang at eight, and she groaned as she reached for it. "Hello," she answered groggily.

I got up from the bed, threw on a T-shirt and shorts, and then went to make us some coffee, even though I wanted to stay in bed, but the caffeine would help start the morning off right. I knew we were supposed to meet Noya in another hour and we still hadn't located another kayak for me to use.

Serena entered the kitchen while I was leaning on the counter and staring off into space. I hadn't fully awakened. The sour expression on her face prompted my question.

"What's up? You look like you lost your best friend."

"Kayaking is canceled. Noya's girlfriend is flying in today, and she has to pick her up from the airport."

I was doing a happy dance. "We can still go or…" I wiggled my eyebrows. "There's always fun and games in the bedroom now that we have the whole day to ourselves. I'll cook us something special to refuel our energies."

Serena was pouting. "It sounds like she's going to try to work things out, and then they'll be off on tour together. I got the brush off. She said she had fun, but with her girlfriend back on the scene, she didn't need me to sit in anymore."

"Well, that's fantastic they're trying to work things out. It's kismet. I was going to talk with you later about this, but I guess now's as good a time as any."

She slumped onto one of the kitchen chairs. "I need coffee first if we're going to have a serious conversation."

"You sit and relax while I whip us up some breakfast."

I poured her a cup of coffee and added cream and sugar just the way I knew she liked it. She sat there in silence while I made my masterpiece.

Hollandaise sauce was extremely tricky to make, but I'd perfected my recipe. I poured it over the eggs benedict, northwest style. The other day, I came across a small fish market and bought smoked salmon, which I placed under the English muffin. The rich pale-yellow sauce was a perfect consistency. I placed the platter in front of her. I wanted everything I made for her to be special.

She took her fork to my masterpiece and cut off a large section, placing it in her mouth and moaning as I suspected the flavor burst on her tongue. "Oh God, that is so good. If you keep cooking for me, I'm gonna end up weighing five hundred pounds."

I looked at her long, lean body and seriously doubted that. I was the one who had to worry about my weight at barely over five feet. "You look perfect to me." I sat down in the other chair at the small table in her kitchen and proceeded to take a bite before it got cold. There is nothing more disgusting than cold eggs benedict.

"Maybe I'll head to the gym today since the kayak trip was canceled."

"Oh, I was hoping you would show me around. I've been tooling around on my own looking for a job, but so far nothing's materialized."

"What?" she asked around a mouthful of food.

"Job. I don't want to take a line cook job. I was hoping for something more upscale, like a sous chef in one of the nicer restaurants, but they all want someone with a culinary degree, and I never finished."

"You're not going to finish respiratory school?"

"I'd rather move here, get a job, and maybe figure that out later. I've got most of my things packed up already. I just need some help to drive here. Alaska is a long way, and I was hoping we could share the driving."

"Whoa, whoa, whoa. I think we need to do some more planning. I'm all for spontaneity, but..." Serena started to say.

I wanted to suck the words back into my mouth and pretend I'd never uttered them.

"You're right of course. This is a big move," I back peddled. "I can't believe I've fallen into the U-Haul trap."

She visibly relaxed. "I really like you, Colette, but Alaska is a very different place, and not everyone enjoys living here, especially living here as a lesbian. Washington is so much more progressive. You should take the time to research things and complete school. You only have one quarter left, and it would be a shame if you didn't finish.

Long-distance relationships can work. We can talk over the phone and plan things out. By then I'll know if the gig with Noya will transpire or not. There still might be an opportunity. It sounded like things were shaky."

I could almost see the air seep out of my balloon of happiness. It was selfish of me, but I didn't want Noya and her girlfriend to split because it might diminish our chances for a successful long-term relationship. I knew I couldn't compete with the chance to join an established band. If I were in her shoes, I'd jump at the chance. That's how musicians rolled.

†

With Noya out of the picture, Serena and I managed to fall into a domestic pattern that, although not exciting like when we first came together, felt comfortable enough. I was still looking for a job on the sly but was smart enough not to broach the subject again. I figured if I found the perfect job, she'd be happy.

After almost a week, Serena genuinely seemed to appreciate coming home to my specially prepared dinners. I was pulling out all the stops. This was something I excelled at. Although I hadn't ever attended culinary school, I'd studied under a few chefs who did have their degrees from reputable institutes.

Ceviche is an easy dish to make, and I'd prepared that when I ran out of time after pounding the pavement looking for a job. When Serena nearly skipped into the kitchen after work, I could tell she was in a great mood.

One thing I'd learned in the past week was that her moods could shift on a dime. One day, she could be tender and loving, and the next, I felt the chill all the way to my bones. On occasion, she was almost disdainful in her interactions.

Serena tossed her bag on the chair in the living room and smiled at me. "Guess what?"

I laughed. "Something good I suspect."

"Oh, my God, not just good. Amazing. Things are going to work out perfectly now."

"Hey, back that amazing train up. What's going to work out perfectly?"

"Noya called me at work today. Her girlfriend has to go back to Florida, so she asked if I can tour with her for the next three months. That will give you time to finish school, and I'll get to follow my dream."

I'm sure my mouth was open, but no words came out.

Serena narrowed her eyes, and her hard expression scared me. "You don't seem happy for me. I would be happy for you."

"When do you have to leave? What about your job?"

She turned to the side and wouldn't look me in the eyes. "Um, that's the only downside. We leave tomorrow. Hey, you can stay here if that's what you're worried about. You know, until your flight back to Washington."

"You can just leave your job?" I repeated my question hoping reality would sink in. It was so irresponsible for her to quit her job and take the chance she could make it as a full-time musician. *Boy, was I the pot calling the kettle black.*

"I can get a job anytime I want, but this is a once in a lifetime opportunity. I work for a stupid real estate office.

It's not like I'm leaving some big career. It's just a job that pays the bills."

I sat heavily in the chair, poured myself a glass of wine, and drank myself into a stupor. We didn't make love that night, and when she left the next day, our goodbye was decidedly frosty.

After Serena left, I paid the extra fees to change my plane ticket and headed back to Washington. We hadn't exactly split, but I could feel the crack in the wood widen.

CHAPTER EIGHTEEN

Melissa

There was an extra bounce in my step as I left work on Wednesday. My staff had been merciless as they teased me about connecting with Christine before I went to the island and left for my annual trek to Victoria.

Mary was coming back from lunch and met me in the hallway. "We want details," she said, "and pictures."

Kim rounded the corner as I was making my escape. "That smile looks good on you. Have fun and do everything I would do—which, by the way, gives you a lot of leeway because this old hippy never holds back."

"See y'all on Tuesday. I'll have my cell phone with me in case you need to contact me."

"We're not calling you on vacation, but I can't make any guarantees with any other of the bozos around here. I was here on the mother-baby unit having my second kid, legs spread wide, and this nurse had the nerve to ask me something about her paycheck."

I stopped in the hall with my bag slung over my shoulder. "You're kidding, right?"

"Nope. Welcome to small-town America," Mary answered.

"I get stopped in Fred Meyer all the time, don't you?" Kim asked.

"Not yet, but I haven't lived here my whole life, and I'm still getting to know all the employees," I answered.

"Maybe you should stay a recluse," Kim joked.

"I'm not a recluse," I defended.

Kim shrugged her shoulders. "Admit it, you scurry away every chance you get. I don't blame you. Not many prospects for hot dates here in Republican Land."

"Hey, I'm a Republican, and besides, some lesbians are Republicans," Mary said.

"Now there's an oxymoron," Kim mumbled.

"I am not getting into a political debate while my long weekend awaits. See you later." I hurried down the hall before the rest of my staff could snag me for any last-minute questions.

Pushing the back door open, I lifted my face to the sun and soaked in the healing rays. Inside my car, I quickly opened the sunroof and turned on the air conditioning. The heat was stifling at first, but at least it would cool enough that by the time I picked up Sarasota and Freud they wouldn't jump around on the burning seats like kitties on a hot tin roof.

Candie had agreed to watch my furbabies over the long weekend, but their cries of pain during the three-hour drive was sure to break my heart. I needed to find a cat sitter and quick if I wanted to be away for more than a couple of days, which was the maximum time I could leave them alone in the chalet. Freud was definitely the louder of the two, but Sarasota added to his chorus of complaints for the first hour.

†

The original plan was to meet Christine for dinner on the way to the island, and then I would connect with Tori and Janet the next morning at the boat. Plans have a way of changing.

In my excitement to see Christine, I hadn't quite worked out all the logistics. I wasn't sure if it was very kind of me to leave my kitties in the car while we had dinner. The west side of the state was a lot cooler than the east, so I knew they wouldn't cook in the car, but they wouldn't be pleased, especially after the two-and-a-half-hour drive to Arlington.

My GPS was spot on and took me to her doorstep without any wrong turns. Sarasota and Freud had finally curled up on the back seat and were napping peacefully. I shut the door carefully, lest I wake the tiny beasts.

Wiping my sweaty hands on my jeans, I knocked lightly and waited. Christine had told me she was coming off a double shift and might take a nap before dinner, so I should just walk in because she would leave the door open. I felt funny doing that, but after a few minutes of awkwardly standing on her doorstep, I turned the knob and quietly entered.

Her golden retriever was lying on a bed, and her eyes opened, but she didn't make another move—not even lifting her head. Clearly not a guard dog. I could have been a psycho lesbian stalker for all she knew.

I discovered Christine stretched out on her couch, sleeping peacefully, and I took a moment to observe her. She had such a beautiful complexion. Rosy high cheekbones, something any woman would kill for. She was gorgeous without a single stitch of makeup. I could tell she'd spent a bit of time outside because her legs and arms had a healthy golden glow.

I felt funny about waking her up, so I waited, hoping she would sense my presence. She didn't. I felt honored she would sacrifice her rest to go out to dinner with me because, clearly, she'd been up now for over twenty-four hours and had to be exhausted.

After five minutes, I squatted down beside her and brushed my hand against her forehead. Her beautiful blue-green eyes slowly opened. She stretched her arms like a cat and said, "Hi, you made it."

"Your golden didn't bark or move from her spot. I guess she's not much of a guard dog."

She chuckled. "Sasha has a thyroid condition. If she opened her eyes upon your arrival, that's her idea of a greeting."

"She's cute. How old?"

"I think she's seven."

"She still has a puppy face."

"That's the chow mixed in with the golden. It gives her that perpetual puppy look, but she also has the stubbornness chows are known for." Christine stood. "Let me go change into pants, and we can leave shortly."

"I had to bring my cats with me. Do you think they'll be okay in the car while we eat?"

"Why don't you bring them inside? Sasha loves cats. Zari, my Persian, might hiss, but he's a big chicken and will run and hide under the bed."

"Are you sure?"

"Of course, I'd love to meet them."

"Neither one has front claws. Although I'd probably never have another cat declawed again after reading about it, they can't do any real damage to Sasha, Zari, or your furniture."

Christine waved her hand in the air. "I'm not concerned."

She followed me outside to my car. I picked up Sarasota who meowed in protest. I suppose she was napping peacefully before I disturbed my spoiled little queen.

"They're beautiful," Christine exclaimed.

I nodded. "And spoiled rotten."

Freud let her pick him up, and we walked back into her house and set them both down. Sasha opened her eyes but didn't move from her bed. They both immediately began sniffing the ground. Sarasota, who was the more assertive of the two, was undoubtedly on the hunt for Zari. She meowed loudly, announcing her presence like she owned the place. She was a haughty little thing sometimes. Making a beeline for the golden, she sniffed and then put her paw on the gentle dog. Sasha snorted but remained in place. *You're just a cat, after all,* I imagined the dog saying to Sarasota's overture of friendship.

When it was clear Sasha wasn't interested in playing, she left her new friend and headed for the staircase, with her

119

brother in tow, and began to climb the stairs. I ventured a glance at Christine, who didn't seem fazed.

"Um, maybe we should follow them to make sure Sarasota behaves herself. Freud is usually mellow, but Sarasota definitely has an attitude."

"Okay, and then I can give you a tour of the place."

My furbabies made a beeline to her bedroom, and I followed squatting down to see what had caught Sarasota's attention. Huddled in the corner was a fluffy black cat hissing up a storm.

"Sarasota, don't corner the poor guy. If you want to make friends, not scare him, be nice."

Freud plopped down next to the bed and waited for his sister to break the ice, his tail flipping lazily back and forth. I was glad his ears weren't back, and the flip of his tail wasn't at double speed. Those were signs of agitation.

Christine put her hand on my back and squatted next to me, peering at the two cats warily acquainting themselves with one another. "They'll be fine. Zari's hiss is bigger than his bite. He's a big old wussy. I'd say pussy, but, well... ya know." She winked at me.

I stood and offered her my hand. "Okay, I'm going to trust you, but if we come back to puffs of hair strategically flying all over the place, I'm blaming you."

She took my hand, and her knees creaked. "Thanks. I played softball when I was younger, and it was a killer on my knees. As for the fur floating in the air, that's what vacuums are for. I have to warn you I'm a bit OCD when it comes to trotting out the vacuum cleaner. I don't like cat litter or fur in places it shouldn't be."

"No problem. I'll feel right at home. My mother is the queen of cleanliness."

She let go of my hand and reminded me, "I promise to supervise the children while I change clothes, and then we can head out."

"Oh, yeah, right, sorry." I could feel my cheeks redden.

I walked down the stairs and sat on the couch with my hands clasped in my lap and my leg shaking up and down. All the nervousness of a first date returned with a vengeance. *Wait, what? First date? Is that how I saw this?* Yeah, who was I kidding? I saw this as a first date.

†

When I heard Christine walk down the stairs, I stood awkwardly waiting for her. She walked into her kitchen and grabbed her keys, stuffing them in her pocket. After she turned around, she took two purposeful steps in my direction and kissed me.

I didn't have time to react other than to lean in and accept the gentle kiss. It wasn't one of those curl your toes, drag the woman to bed, kind of kisses, but then I wouldn't have wanted that at this point. I appreciated that she hadn't rammed her tongue in my mouth or slobbered all over me. Just a nice sweet kiss.

I suppose that was the defining moment regarding whether this would end up being a date or merely a friendly dinner. Our conversations over the last week were moving into the more personal territory, and I knew I was giving her mixed signals.

I'd been honest about enjoying our daily e-mails and my excitement about seeing her for dinner. I was surprised when in the last e-mail I confessed, "I still want to take the necessary time to heal, but it would be terribly dishonest of me if I didn't tell you I am interested. Your kindness and gentle, open spirit have been such a gift, and I wanted you to know that! I got you a card today that I would like to send, but I don't know where to send it to. I guess I can always hand-deliver it, but it can be so much fun to get mail."

It was a nice kiss. I smiled, and she did the same. Christine was an attractive woman, but when she smiled, she moved into the definitive gorgeous category.

"The sushi restaurant I'm taking you to is close by so you can get on the road and arrive on the island at a reasonable hour. I'd love to take you to my favorite sushi place, but that's farther away."

"Maybe another time."

"You're gonna love it." She grinned.

If she was nervous, I couldn't tell because she seemed so self-assured.

I knew I was nervous and acting particularly goofy for a forty-five-year-old woman. I realized I didn't know the first thing about dating. All my other relationships seemed to evolve organically. In my experience, lesbians got together and were a couple in a matter of hours. Sure, we went out to dinner, had coffee, saw movies, but that was usually after we'd established residency with one another.

Colette and I slept together the night of my breakup with Tristen, the drummer in their old band. Lanie had called that night and told Collette to leave me alone. She wanted Collette to let Tristen and I work out our issues without her interference. Tristan's admission that she had kissed Colette initiated a series of confessions that ultimately ended in Tristan leaving.

I don't know why I let it happen. I guess I felt crappy about Tristen not wanting me anymore and confessing her love for Lanie. I didn't often allow my vulnerability to come to the surface, but I did that night. It hurt, and Colette was the balm for my gaping wound of oozing insecurity. Who knew we'd spend the next eight years together after that night.

Lesbians were such an incestuous bunch. The band with Lanie, Tristen, and Colette was the center of our gang's extracurricular activities. Bridget and I were devoted girlfriends, and the band had a small following of lesbians that were our posse of friends we affectionately called, "the gang." I felt particularly slutty because I'd slept with two of the three band members.

I was determined to have a nice date with Christine, but no way was I going to sleep with her. That was a dangerous pattern I needed to avoid because whenever I slept with a woman, I spent the next several years of my life in relative domestic bliss until they decided it was time to move on to a new shinier model. Famous last words.

†

Christine and I sat in a booth at the restaurant and ordered a sushi platter to share. I was delighted she enjoyed my favorite ethnic cuisine, at least in my mind I'd labeled sushi as ethnic fare. I looked closely at her as she fidgeted in her chair. She was nervous. I could see the telltale signs.

We both picked a bit at the platter of fish set before us and left a fair number of the fresh delicacies on the plate. I suspected our nerves were the culprit and not the food.

I don't recall whether it was high-quality sushi, but I don't think it was awful. I would have remembered that. I remember feeling disappointed the food came so quickly because, despite our nervousness, we were having a nice conversation sprinkled with bouts of laughter that intermittently broke the tension.

"I wish I'd been there to see you at your picnic in that formal attire, all wet…" She wiggled her eyebrows.

"There are pictures."

"Ooh, pictures. Who do I need to bribe to get my hands on the evidence?"

"We had to improvise because the dunk tank wasn't available. It was hysterical standing there while the kids threw the water balloons at us. Some of them had quite the arms, and it stung."

"Whose idea was it to use water balloons?"

I raised my hand. "We'd already plastered the hospital with flyers about the event, what else could I do? We had to come up with plan B."

Christine chuckled. "No that's brilliant. I love the way you think on your feet. You're probably one of those, never give up, kind of people. That's admirable."

"My dad says I'm so hard headed I don't need that bike helmet I wear. He thinks he's funny. I get focused sometimes, and that can be a really bad thing. I prefer to think of myself as persistent and driven, versus obsessive and neurotic."

"Most people I know are obsessive about something. We all have our pet issues or quirks."

"At least you're a Democrat. I'm an open-minded person, but I don't think I could ever date a Republican. That's a quirk I don't think I could ever accept."

Christine laughed. "Ditto."

I didn't want the date to end, but I didn't know how to navigate this uncharted territory. Yes, I was firmly categorizing the dinner as a date now. When the waitress delivered the check to the table, we both knew the evening was, unfortunately, coming to an end.

I grabbed the check. "I asked, let me pay please."

"Only if you let me take you to my favorite sushi place another time and I pay then."

I reluctantly agreed. It was something I was working on. Allowing a partnership to be more balanced. I didn't have to always be the one in control and pay all the time. Besides, this meant we would have another date.

†

When we returned to her house, I started to search for my furbabies. It was late, and I knew I wouldn't get to the island until after midnight.

"Would you like some coffee or tea? It might help with the drive."

"Yeah, I better. I'm more tired than I thought I would be."

"Why don't you stay the night and leave in the morning? I'm worried about you driving this late at night, especially since you told me you're an early riser. This must be the time you usually head to bed."

"On a normal day, I'd already be in bed by now. Although, lately, I haven't been able to sleep very well. Heartbreak is hell on your sleep patterns." *Damn, why did I have to say that?*

Christine gathered me in her arms, and her hug was warm and comforting. "Stay the night, please? I'd like it if you drove in the morning, instead."

"Okay. I can do that. Let me call Tori and Janet, and ask when is the latest I can meet them." I repeated the mantra, *I'm not going to have sex with her*, three times. At that moment, I believed I wouldn't.

I went into the bathroom with a T-shirt and shorts in my hand and changed from my jeans. Christine had clothes in her hands, and as she passed me, she teased, "Normally, I sleep in the nude."

I swallowed hard. This was going to be a long night. To give myself something to do besides awkwardly stare after Christine, I peered under the bed, and all three cats looked up at me. Sarasota had managed to inch closer to Zari who was keeping his distance, but I suspect the hissing had stopped long ago.

"Are they still working out the pecking order?" Christine asked.

My head smacked against the bedframe. "Ouch." I stood and then rubbed the back of my head.

"Sorry, I didn't mean to startle you. Let me take a look." She materialized next to me and gently probed the back of my head. Her light touch sent shivers down my back, and I forgot all about the bump.

126

"Um, it's fine. Remember, I'm particularly hard headed. I suppose pets are a lot like their owners. Sarasota isn't giving up. She's bound and determined to befriend Zari. Freud isn't participating until Sarasota manages to break through Zari's barriers."

CHAPTER NINETEEN

Sarasota

My pleas of agony weren't getting me anywhere, so I stopped after about an hour. Freud, the big baby, kept caterwauling, disturbing my sleep until he eventually shut his big trap.

I had been peacefully sleeping when Melissa finally stopped, so I barely opened my eyes when she got out of the car. I figured this was a potty stop or something, and we'd be on our way again to God knows where. Melissa seemed happy, and that was a welcome change, so I went along without too much protest. Okay, maybe I protested a little in the beginning, but Freud was worse.

A few minutes later, Melissa disturbed my peaceful nap, and there was another woman with her. I was glad when my human picked me up, and the strange woman lifted Freud from the seat where he'd curled up. Freud never did uphold the standards for cat aloofness. The big goof let anyone pick him up as long as they scratched under his chin. She must have known the secret or maybe Melissa had told her. She did say we were beautiful, and that earned her big points in my mind, but not big enough to let her pick me up. I had to be cautious for both of us. She might be good for Melissa, or she might not. Freud wasn't a good judge of character.

When Melissa set me down in the strange house, I saw the big golden dog first. *A dog! A dog! Yippee.* I loved dogs. I never understood why they didn't want to befriend me. Their loss. This one must have been on drugs, though, because she barely moved when I did my little sniffing thing, then placed my paw on her in friendship. Freud always said that wasn't the way you were supposed to greet a dog, but I wasn't gonna stick my butt in her face. How unladylike.

Maybe the dog was sick. I lifted my head and caught a whiff of something. Cat. There was another cat nearby. I looked over at Freud and did my tail swish to let him know he should follow me and started up the big staircase. I was gonna sniff out the competition and let that cat know who was boss. If Melissa was planning on moving us again, I needed to establish that right from the start.

When Colette had brought home those dogs, I'd let them know first thing that even though I liked dogs, they were not the boss of me. Red was cool, but Blackie needed a few bats on the head before he learned. I missed Red and Blackie.

They were both dumb drooling dogs, but we had fun together. I'd smack them on the nose and then run and climb up on the top of the counter taunting them. Oh yeah, those were the good old days.

Bedrooms were famous places for cats to hide, so I made a beeline for the open room with a big mahogany bed. There he was. Wow, he was a big, fat, furry, black cat. I knew that a lot of people thought black cats were bad luck or something, but that was stupid superstition. I would be the bigger feline and introduce myself, let the cat know I wasn't some dumbass narrow-minded Himalayan who looked down my nose at black cats. Besides, he looked like he was a Persian cat, so definitely someone I should associate with. Himalayans, like Freud and I, were an elite class, but Persians came darn close to our refined breeding. When he hissed at us, I inched closer.

Melissa warned, "Sarasota, don't corner the poor guy. If you want to make friends, not scare him, be nice."

Hmff. I knew what I was doing. When a cat goes into another cat's territory, an assertive greeting is the only way to establish the pecking order.

Freud plopped down behind me, letting me do all the hard work. What a chicken shit. Boys. Sheesh. I kept inching closer, and the black fuzzball hissed again but stood his ground in the corner watching warily.

Oh goody. This was my favorite game. The cat who blinks first loses. I was a master at this. I met his eyes and refused to look away. When the strange woman said, "They'll be fine. Zari's hiss is bigger than his bite. He's just a big old wussy. I'd say pussy, but well… ya know," I knew I was gonna win this one.

I heard Melissa respond, "Okay, I'm trusting you, but if we come back to tufts of hair strategically flying all over the place, I'm blaming you."

As if, humph, I would let another cat pull out my beautiful fur.

I will admit I got a little nervous when Melissa exited the room, and she left us with that strange woman rooting around in her drawers. But I refused to turn my head and lose the staring contest.

Bingo. After the woman left, Zari, that's what the woman had called him, turned his head and looked away first. I settled in and began my wait. It sounded like Melissa was going out, and I was gonna make sure I prevailed on establishing who was top cat. I almost felt sorry for Zari because even after they left, he didn't budge from his little corner under the bed. I caught a few winks while my human was away. Ah, such is the life of a top cat.

CHAPTER TWENTY

Melissa

I waited until Christine crawled under the covers and then I joined her. We were facing one another and, like two magnets, came together for a goodnight kiss. That was all I had planned on doing.

The touches started out innocently enough. Christine moved her hand under my T-shirt and began stroking my back. It was damn near impossible to control my reaction to her touch. When her hand brushed against the side of my breast, I decided the hell with it. I was a forty-five-year-old woman, and if I wanted to have sex, I would throw caution to the wind.

When her hand moved to my outer thigh, grazing the edge of my buttocks, I wasn't able to mask my reaction. I was sure Christine knew exactly what she was doing, and I wanted more.

I lifted my T-shirt over my head and tossed it to the side. She followed suit. We still had our shorts to create one last barrier, in case we decided to stop and wait.

Her fingertips moved along my ribcage. "How much weight have you lost?" she asked the concern evident in her voice.

"About ten to fifteen pounds. I know I need to add a few pounds. I probably look like a scarecrow."

"No, you're beautiful, but you are a bit underweight. Eastern medicine always recommends you carry about ten extra pounds so that you have reserves for when you get sick. It seems like you could easily gain twenty." She continued to stroke my sides and back.

When her leg slipped between mine, we started to move together, and I was definitely becoming more and more aroused by her body against my own.

My shorts were loose, which made it easy for her to slip her hand inside and tentatively touch the outer edges of my lips. I was already starting to drip.

A surge went through my body when I felt the light brush against my clit. I had the overwhelming need to touch her back. I started with a light caress to her large milky white breasts. She had glorious breasts. I was usually attracted to women with a bit of meat on their bones, and Christine was perfect. She wasn't overweight, but she wasn't like me, skin and bones.

As she continued to tease me, I moved my mouth to her nipple and sucked. Christine moaned, and I discovered her breasts were ultrasensitive.

Our bodies shifted, and we found a position that enabled both of us to dip into each other's wet center. She moved her thumb up and down over my clit as a single finger slid inside. I was glad she hadn't attempted to enter me with more than one finger because I was very small and generally didn't enjoy too much inside.

Even though I had a desperate craving to taste her, I was lost in the feelings as our awakening grew. We were in perfect sync. The symphony of moans blended with the jazz music she'd put on and was playing lightly in the background.

I was a relatively vocal lover and didn't mind when my partner expressed her delight as well. The vocalizations often sent me even further into the stratosphere. I hoped Christine enjoyed hearing my moans and words of encouragement.

"Oh, that feels so good," I ventured.

"Tell me what you like," she responded.

"This is good. I like a light touch and not a lot inside."

We continued to touch each other and move together.

"I'm close. I want to come together," Christine whispered.

It always spurred on my arousal when my partner was close. So, that was all it took for me to reach the precipice of final release.

"Oh yes."

When I felt her contractions, my own body went over the edge, and I felt each pulse match Christine's.

She found my mouth and kissed me gently. "I'm going to miss talking to you over the next five days."

"Come to Victoria," I blurted out.

She pulled back and looked at me. "Really?"

I nodded. "Yes." I realized I wanted to share Victoria with her, and I wanted Tori and Janet to meet her.

"I can't come tomorrow with you, but maybe I can find a way to get there by Saturday."

"There's a float plane that flies into the harbor, or you could take the Victoria Clipper from Seattle."

"A float plane might be a lot of fun." She smiled.

"I'll meet you and then bring you back to the boat."

The annual trek to Victoria was turning into a better trip than I had originally envisioned. I was sure I would feel like a fifth wheel because Colette wasn't joining us this year, but now that I had someone to vacation with, the distraction would take me away from memories of our trips together. Sometimes it was good when tradition shifted. There was nothing wrong with creating new memories and new traditions.

†

After I dropped off Sarasota and Freud, I rushed to the marina where we moored our boat. It was a gorgeous day as I carried my bag down the weather-beaten path to our slip. I was careful not to trip on the uneven planks as I nearly skipped down B dock.

I saw the plume of smoke revealing that the diesel motor was coughing out the initial toxins as the boat warmed up sufficiently before we attempted to putter out to sea.

"Sorry, sorry," I said as I tossed my bag on the stern and hopped on board.

"You look like the cat that ate the canary," Tori remarked. "Was she good?"

I could feel my goofy grin. "Shush. Okay, what can I do?"

135

"We're all set. Just untie the lines and jump on the bow, monkey girl."

I grinned. Tori had nicknamed me monkey girl because I was so nimble and able to jump on and off, navigate untying and tying the lines while she drove the boat in and out of the slip. We were a well-oiled machine, and my role was always to give a push off and jump on board at the last possible moment.

I stepped off the boat and onto the dock. Each line I undid, I tossed to Janet and then held onto the rail at the bow of the boat.

"Are we good to go?"

Tori was at the helm and nodded.

I gave a little push and then swung my body onto the bow like a gymnast ending their routine. Tori slowly motored out of the harbor, and I did my nimble monkey girl thing, gathering the lines and pulling in the bumpers.

Janet stuck her head out of the hatch and took the lines from me. She had a special way of wrapping them, and we'd learned to appreciate the amount of care she took with everything on the boat. Her methods kept everything neat and organized. Next to my mom, Janet was the most organized, clean freak I'd ever met. I appreciated that about her. The *clean freak* was an endearing descriptor.

Tori always drove the boat in and out of the dock and would only let someone else take over for a short bit while in the open waters. We let her because, quite frankly, she was the only one who could navigate in the small areas without smashing into other boats. Boats don't have brakes, and it's damn hard to motor them into the narrow slips, especially when the wind and currents are acting up.

Swinging down into the open hatch, I made my way to the stern and grabbed the folding chair to relax in the sunshine. The breeze, as Tori kicked up the motor to cruising speed, flowed over my face as I settled into the protected corner of the boat.

I closed my eyes and was enjoying the salty air when Janet tapped my shoulder. "The boss says it's time to come inside and tell us what's going on."

"Yeah, get your ass inside and spill," Tori yelled over the motor.

I groaned as I pushed up out of the chair and followed Janet into the protected area where Tori's eyes focused on the water making sure we didn't hit a deadhead. Deadheads were large pieces of wood that could play hell on the prop. She ventured a glance in my direction before returning to the gentle waves. It was a perfect day for travel. The Strait of Juan de Fuca was uncharacteristically calm.

"Nosy Nelly," I said.

"Hey, I left you alone for a full two hours. I think I've exercised tremendous restraint," Tori replied.

Janet looked at me sympathetically. "I tried to get her to leave you be and let you tell us in your own good time, but you know Tori."

"I met someone on Match."

Tori threw her fist in the air. "Yeah, baby. See I told you. The stigma of online dating is almost nonexistent now."

"Yeah, try to tell that to my mom. She'll have a coronary if she finds out. I plan on telling her we met on a bike ride. It's not exactly a lie. We did meet in person for the first time on a bike ride."

"Okay, give us the particulars. You know, how old, what does she do for a living, is she good in bed." Janet smacked Tori on the arm. "What? Don't tell me you're not dying to know."

"Fifty-one, research scientist, and none of your fucking business."

"Ooh, you did sleep with her. Okay, I'm impressed with the scientist thing. You need an intelligent woman who will be your equal. I like that she's older. Probably means she's more settled. When do we get to meet her?"

"Saturday," I mumbled.

"Oh, this keeps getting better and better. So… you invited her to Victoria, did you?"

"It's okay, isn't it?"

"Of course, it is," Janet added.

"You know you can't officially start dating her until she passes our inspection," Tori stated.

"Don't listen to her." Janet threw a cautioning look in Tori's direction.

"I do kinda want your impression. Obviously, I suck at picking out long-term girlfriends. They always seem to want to dump me after several years. I honestly thought Colette and I would make it after the five-year mark passed. When we'd made it over the seven-year itch, I thought it would be smooth sailing. Christine is very different from all my other partners."

"Yeah, like she has a steady job and isn't dependent on you to support her," Tori said with a hint of bitterness in her voice.

"Can we not talk about Colette?"

"Good idea. Tell us more about Christine. That's her name, right?"

"Yeah. She came out here to attend school at Bastyr and has a Master's in acupuncture and oriental medicine."

"That sounds fascinating." Janet grabbed her water and took a swig.

"Hey, babe, want to grab me another beer?" Tori held up her Rolling Rock.

"Sure." Janet went out to the back where we kept the large cooler.

"So, you had sex, didn't you? I can see it on your face."

I'm sure my face turned bright red. "Yeah, I guess I'm a bit of a slut, huh?"

"Nope. I thought you tossed away that good Catholic upbringing years ago." Tori laughed.

"Nah, once a Catholic, always a Catholic—the guilt keeps giving and giving."

Janet came back in, handed Tori a beer, and then sat. "Tell us more about this new woman in your life, and no, don't let Tori goad you into giving up the intimate details. There are more important things to learn about her than that."

For the rest of the way to Victoria, I told my two best friends about Christine.

CHAPTER TWENTY-ONE

Colette

When I returned to Washington, I swallowed my pride and begged my way back into the respiratory program with plans to finish my final quarter. I still had some time off before the fall quarter started. Since I was dangerously low on cash, I made the sacrifice and put my motorcycle up for sale. The little bit of cash I had remaining from my mom's estate wasn't going to last long, especially since I wasn't working full-time. I picked up shifts here and there as a respiratory assistant, but that barely covered my rent.

Serena and I talked on the phone every couple of days, and she sounded happy. I didn't think much about the fact that I always called her. There was no mention of future plans for us, but there wasn't a definitive end to our relationship, either. I knew it wasn't smart to push the issue, but one night, I had to know where we were heading, so I broached the topic.

"Serena, can we talk about us?"

I could hear the pause on the other end of the phone.

"Look, Colette, I like you, but maybe we're going a little too fast."

"You were the one who asked me to come to Alaska. You said you knew a drummer, and I thought we were going to try to start a band."

"I know. I let my excitement for that possibility overtake any common sense. The drummer moved with a band before I could ask her and then this thing with Noya took form. Things are different now that I'm touring."

"Maybe I could join the band too. Four people generate a richer sound. I can play keyboards, mandolin and have also been a backup drummer."

"If it were up to me, I'd say yes, but when you add a fourth, the money has to be split four ways, and since she's doing well with only three, why would she want to lower her profits. You understand, right?"

"Not really. I'm in love with you and willing to make sacrifices for us, but it doesn't seem like you're as willing to meet me half way."

"Whoa, love. I never said I loved you. Sure, we connect and have great sex, but I'm not ready for the U-Haul. When I asked if you wanted to come to Alaska and play music, I didn't mean we would get married or anything. I'm still young and am definitely not ready to settle down. I understand you're at that point in your life. Cause you're gonna turn forty soon, right?"

"Next year, I'll be forty-one," I mumbled.

"See, I'm not even thirty yet. Way too young to be committed to just one person."

"You're seeing other people…" I choked out.

"Oh, honey, you thought we were exclusive? I'm sorry I didn't make that clear. Um… this is awkward. Like I said before, I like you, and we have a good time together, but you're a little too needy for me. Maybe we should cool it for a bit. We can get together when I visit Mom… um…"

"Don't bother." I slammed down the phone, and that was the last time I talked with Serena.

I realized I had thrown away an eight-year relationship for what? A fantasy. Did I want to repair things with Melissa if that was possible? I honestly didn't know. I'd violated her trust, so I wasn't sure it was feasible.

The long Labor Day weekend trip was coming up, and I was sure Melissa was out on our boat with Tori and Janet. Our boat. No, it wasn't our boat anymore, and in reality, it never was. Melissa owned everything, I was just a passenger. But I'd left Melissa for a romp in the sac and a dream that Serena and I would form a band and ride off into the sunset. Now I wasn't even a passenger.

I leaned back on my bed in the loft and let my tears flow. I was a fool and Karma had made its presence known. The hardest lessons in life were always the most painful. Karma was indeed a vengeful bitch.

✝

The next day, I called my older sister, Daria, who lived in Seattle to see if she wanted to do something over the long weekend. She never judged. Although she had liked Melissa and thought she was good for me, she supported my decision to end the relationship, believing Serena was my soulmate.

"Hello."

"Hey," I answered.

"You sound down. What's up?" Daria asked.

"Serena and I broke up last night."

"Oh, sorry, hon. What can I do?"

"I was hoping you didn't have plans this weekend and maybe we could do something. I feel a little lost right now."

"Do you think maybe you and Melissa can work things out?"

"Oh, I don't know. I really hurt her."

"Do you want to?"

"We still had problems to work through, and now I've pretty much added a whole heaping pile of shit to them." I crossed my legs and settled in for a long conversation.

"I sent her a book."

"What?"

"I knew how destroyed she would be, so I found this book with Buddhist sayings. A little Zen philosophy. It helped me when Yvette left."

I blew out a big breath. "I never knew that."

"I know. I didn't want you to think I didn't support you. I liked Melissa. I thought she was good for you. Maybe your relationship is still salvageable. Do you know if she went to Victoria for the long weekend?"

"Yeah, she did. I called Candie yesterday to check on the dogs, and she told me she'd dropped off the cats. Red was especially happy to see Sarasota. She's his buddy. She let the dogs in when Red started crying at the window after seeing Sarasota saunter by."

Daria laughed. "Sarasota is a sassy little thing. You should give Melissa a few days and then maybe go to Cle Elum and talk with her. I'd suggest you do that face to face. Maybe go up to her place next weekend."

"I'll think about it. Can you get away? Maybe we can go to Bumbershoot on Saturday or Sunday. I haven't been in years."

"That sounds like fun. I wish you were playing again."

"The competition is particularly stiff now and hard for a solo act."

"Yeah, but you're better than most of those small venues."

"Thanks for the vote of confidence. I'll take a look at the line-up and see which day we should go."

"Okay. Do you want to come for dinner tonight?"

"Sure, that sounds great. Thanks, Daria. I'll talk to you later."

†

I was beginning to question my quest for a music career as a real option. I liked the notion of helping people, and when I'd decided on respiratory school, it was because that was a practical career, but it didn't exactly feed my soul. When I first started back to school, I'd toyed with the idea of obtaining an English degree. Writing was another passion of mine, and I thought maybe an English degree would help. I'd attended a writing workshop after winning a spot in the short story competition. My short, *Blue Jello*, was a story loosely based on my experience caring for my mother when she was dying of ovarian cancer. The dream took form after receiving accolades on the story.

I grabbed my laptop and decided to expand *Blue Jello*. I was going to write an entire novel about my experiences with my mother. Although it was certainly a serious topic, there were humorous parts to expand on, like when we forgot to grab the urn and bring Mom to the church for her last goodbye to the world.

I was in the car when Daria asked, "Did you grab the urn?"

After a quick double check with the rest of my sisters and brother, we learned no one had thought to retrieve the urn from the mantle.

"Shit," I exclaimed. "We forgot Mom."

Daria made a quick U-turn, and Mom was indeed late for her own funeral. Melissa was pacing in the church foyer. She didn't know anyone but my family. Hanging with strangers was something that made Melissa very nervous.

"Sorry, sorry." I grabbed her hand, and we ran to the first pew.

"What happened?" she whispered.

"We forgot Mom," I answered.

She squeezed my hand. Melissa was like a duck out of water. She wasn't sure how to support me, so she drew back into herself and became more introverted. I knew she wanted to help me during this time, but I never felt like she understood. I had to admit that whenever I asked, she was right there by my side. A quiet sentinel. But I wanted to talk things through, and she was clearly uncomfortable. Melissa was a fixer.

Her mom told her once that she possessed the masculine tendency to want to fix things, and sometimes a woman just wanted to talk. She'd advised her to listen without offering solutions. Melissa tried, but I don't think she quite got there all the time.

It was time to write that novel. I'd wanted to do it for years, and now I had both the time and the inspiration. One thing Melissa was always good at was supporting whatever endeavor I chose to pursue.

She'd worked tirelessly on my website and the cover to my CD. We didn't have money for a sound person, so she took abuse when we barked out orders to bring up the mid or lower the treble. She was the one who engineered the speaker stands and lugged all the equipment out of the back of the truck because I have a bad back. Not once did she ever complain as she hauled the seventy-five-pound speakers into the various venues.

So why had I left her in the dust? That was something I would have to ponder on this long Labor Day weekend before I could talk to her and try to figure out where it all went astray.

CHAPTER TWENTY-TWO

Melissa

Tori and Janet were at their favorite restaurant, ordering Bellinis as soon as the clock struck twelve. I told them I would meet them later for dinner after I picked up Christine from the dock. Her plane was due to come in at one.

I found a flower shop and tightly held a single red rose in my hand. My heart was pounding hard in my chest as the plane touched down on the water. The city was already alive with activity. Wood boats were gleaming in the harbor, and although they were the same ones we saw every year, we loved walking through their polished wood. The owners clearly took pride in their lustrous hulls and shiny brass fixtures.

I knew Christine loved boats, but she was more of a sailboat or kayak kind of person, and I wanted her to like our power boat as much as a sailboat. I didn't think I could ever muster enough energy to maintain a sailboat. The power boat was temperamental enough. We'd often joked that boats were big holes their owners threw money into. It was true—there was always something.

Christine stepped off the plane and onto the dock. Her smile matched the sparkle of the sun on the water. She repositioned her backpack, and when she approached, I awkwardly thrust the rose in her face.

"Thank you."

We did a kind of weird dance and then finally figured out a way to hug one another. I was in rare form. How I ever managed to get anyone to want to ask me on a second date was a mystery to me.

"How was your trip?" I asked. This seemed a safe topic.

She smiled broadly. "It was glorious. I've never been on a float plane before. Coming into the harbor was so beautiful. I recommend it."

I thought back to my trip to Stehekin with Colette and mumbled, "Been there, done that, and don't want to do it again."

She looked perplexed.

"I'm not one for small airplanes. I imagine in my head that the pilot will turn around and offer a beverage and that's just wrong," I clarified.

"So, you have a fear of flying?" she asked.

"Sort of. I barely handle the big jets; small planes send me into a tailspin. I'd rather drive or take a boat even if it takes four times as long."

"Good to know." She blessed me with that amazing smile again.

I pointed to her bag. "I'm glad you travel light. We can walk back to the boat and drop that off if you want. Then we can cruise around to see the wooden boats and catch the street performers."

She slipped her arm into the left strap to secure the bag on her back and moved the rose to her left hand. When I pivoted to the right to walk down the dock, she let her right hand casually meet my left and clasped them together as our fingers interlocked.

I loved holding hands. Colette and I hadn't done that often enough in my humble opinion. To me, it was a symbol of simple love and respect. There wasn't anything remotely sexual about holding hands, but the feel of another woman's fingers intertwined between mine always left me with a peaceful, loving feeling. That sounded like a song. I think it was the partial lyrics to one of those oldies I sometimes listened to.

I'd only felt comfortable enough to do that in public in the last couple of years. I'm not sure how relaxed Colette felt about public displays of affection. The nineties were an improvement over the eighties, but an out and proud lesbian still suffered the disapproving looks and an occasional taunt from others. It was usually more than I wanted to deal with, and I definitely got the sense Colette was more reluctant than I was. So, we restrained ourselves in public. It had bled over into our private life, I suppose. I was determined not to make that same mistake. I felt overt affection for Christine, and I was serious about showing it.

"Wow, this is a beautiful place. I've always wanted to come here," Christine said as we strolled along at a leisurely pace.

When we reached the boat, her eyes traveled over the surface. The glossy white hull sparkled against the deep blue of the water. I led her inside, and before she said anything, I got the impression she thought our boat was nice.

After I took her bag and set it on the bed, I pulled open the refrigerator and retrieved a bottle of water. "Can I get you something to drink?"

"Water sounds great to me. It's hotter up here than I thought it would be. Your boat is beautiful. I've never been on a power boat before. Only a sailboat in the West Indies."

"I'm too lazy to sail. I prefer to push the throttle forward and be done with it."

Christine laughed. "I can sail, but the boat was chartered. It was the most glorious two weeks I can ever remember having. I decided to treat myself after the friends of mine started to engage in some destructive behavior I wanted no part of."

I raised my eyebrows.

"I left the drug scene a long time ago, and they didn't. It nearly killed me. I've been more than twenty years sober and clean."

Shit on a shingle. Colette was an alcoholic, and I didn't want a repeat of what I'd just been through with her. Christine didn't seem at all like Colette. She was definitely comfortable in her skin, and I suspected this was a dragon she'd slain long ago.

I sat in the booth at the table and took a swig of my water but didn't comment.

"Sorry, I guess I just blurted that out. Are you worried?"

"Um, no…" I hedged.

"Look, I'm not proud of where I've been, but I'm nothing like I was, and I work hard to keep it that way. Alcohol was never my drug of choice. Cocaine was, and I have zero craving for the stuff anymore. I haven't for a very long time. I'm not judging. I just didn't want to be around it."

"Thanks for being so honest with me. Colette was an alcoholic, and well, she fell off the wagon. It caused issues."

"Addiction is a tough disease. I feel for her and her attempt at recovery."

That was the kind of person Christine was—loving, kind, and accepting of people's flaws. I could take a few pages from her book. I wanted to be supportive of Colette, but all I ever seemed to do was toss out ultimatums. I'd told her I wouldn't stay in a relationship with an active alcoholic. Of course, I'd never followed through on that threat. She beat me to the punch and dumped me. I was sure alcohol was part of her life again. She was convinced a drink or two was okay. Her therapist, according to her, had said so.

"Ready to go out and see the wooden boats?" I asked. The message in my mind was that it was time to change the subject because this one wasn't something I wanted to talk about. She took the cue.

"Sure, I'd love to. Lead the way, beautiful."

We ducked our heads and emerged from below, squinting into the bright sunshine. I locked the cabin, and once again, we strolled down the dock hand in hand.

†

We met up with my friends at a nice restaurant. Besides Tori and Janet, there was another couple we sometimes connected with in Victoria. They had a gorgeous tugboat. One was a retired real estate mogul and the other a former dental hygienist. I don't think they were strapped for money.

Christine was nervous. I don't believe they had intended to send her into orbit with their questions, but it felt more like a grilling than normal dinner conversation.

"So, I have this friend who once had someone perform cupping therapy on her. What do you think about that?" the real estate mogul asked.

Christine's leg bounced up and down, and when she answered, gone was the bright smile. "Cupping can be very powerful but has to be administered correctly for it to have the right benefits for the patient."

"Do you offer cupping therapy?"

"No, I don't have an active practice now."

There was something sad about her response. I knew she had a license to practice acupuncture in Maryland, but not in Washington. It sounded like she'd given up that dream for a steady job in healthcare.

"Okay, no more grilling, please." I stepped in to rescue Christine.

My halibut magically appeared, along with everyone else's dinner, and we all moaned with pleasure. Whoever had recommended this place should receive a medal. After one bite of my fish, I couldn't believe the burst of flavor. The chef had cooked the halibut to perfection, and I was sure I would never have as good a meal anywhere else. Fish was hard to get right, but they'd accomplished that feat with ease.

"How's the halibut?" Christine whispered.

"Oh, my God, so good. How's your steak?"

She took a bite of her meat. After chewing the small morsel, she sighed. "Perfection. Everything is perfection."

"Even my nosy friends?"

She smiled. "It's okay. I was nervous and wanted to make a good impression. I don't think I did very well. It's the same with interviews. I get all stiff and then clipped in my answers to questions."

I set my fork down and stroked her thigh. "You're not interviewing for a job here, and the only opinion that ultimately matters is mine. You've already passed my tests. You had me at clip-on pedals."

She chuckled. "You're far too easy to please."

"Hey, you two, no more whispering sweet nothings into each other's ears," Tori blurted out.

Janet smacked her on the arm. "Stop embarrassing them."

Random conversation about a variety of topics filled the rest of the evening. They had thankfully turned their focus elsewhere, and Christine relaxed. Both of us were relatively quiet, letting the extroverts control the conversation.

After dinner, my friends let us walk slowly behind to give us some privacy. We met them back at the boat and settled in for the evening. Since we were all early risers, we crawled into our respective beds and crashed. There might have been a small amount of touching. But with Tori and Janet so close by, I felt weird thrashing around and letting my voice of passion ring into the small cabin below where they would tease us mercilessly the next day.

†

Even though we had a full shower on the boat, the normal ritual for getting ready in the morning was to have at least one cup of coffee, then a quick brush of our teeth. Like campers, we used our bottled water for that. The marina had excellent facilities, so we would carry our bath bags for a long hot shower and bypass the tiny bathroom in the boat.

Sunday was our ritual day for brunch, but I guess Tori and Janet figured we'd be hungry for something else. After coffee, they scrambled away to take a very early shower and left us alone in the cabin.

Tori's parting comment was, "Hey, why don't we meet you two at our brunch place at 11:30. I'll make the reservations." She waved, then winked before exiting. "Have fun this morning."

I suppose it doesn't matter if a person is eighteen, forty-five, or fifty-one, when in that new love stage. Christine and I followed suit and couldn't get enough of each other.

I grinned at her. "Well, that wasn't too obvious."

"I take it they don't usually leave for the shower this early."

I laughed. "Not even close. We sit around and have several cups while we read magazines and talk about what we want to do for the day. It's a normal Sunday ritual. None of us would even think about making a move until we've slurped our second cup."

"Well, it seems like we have at least three hours to kill. What shall we do?" Christine jumped on the bed, then laid back and put her hands behind her head.

I crawled up her body and kissed her. It began as a gentle, tentative overture and quickly turned almost desperate. It was like if I didn't have her naked and squirming in the next thirty seconds, something dire was about to happen.

Her arms wrapped around my back and held me tight as she began to rub up and down and venture under the waistband of my shorts. Seconds later, she was carefully pulling my T-shirt over my head, and I wasn't offering the least bit of resistance.

"Yours too," I ordered, my voice husky.

She kissed the tip of my nose and then rolled me over before she sat on me and removed her own shirt. Our breasts came together, hers large, soft pillows, while mine were tiny leftover remnants from my drastic loss of weight over the last several months. It didn't matter because it felt exciting to experience skin on skin.

We began to move together, and the motion definitely started our motors running. I had a sudden urge to taste Christine and flipped her over. I began my descent down her body and was grateful for her choice of sleepwear. She was wearing a loose pair of YMCA shorts and no underwear.

I brought my hands to the sides and began pulling her shorts down as I continued to stroke the outside of her thighs while removing the last bit of clothing that was between me and my prize.

Christine's hair was a mix of blonde and gray and gloriously thick and wavy. I loved running my hands through her mane. Her pubic hair was a different texture. It hadn't turned gray yet. The short curly hair wound closely against her outer lips.

I started to kiss my way up her right inner thigh as my left hand grazed her left thigh. I didn't want any part of her body neglected in the pursuit of my current craving. Using my thumbs, I gently parted her lips. I could detect the musky smell and inhaled the glorious aroma. The scent filled my nostrils with joy as I recognized her arousal.

The minute my tongue took its first teasing taste of the tip of her clit, Christine let me hear her appreciation for what I was doing.

"Mmmmm, you can continue doing that for, oh, how about an eternity?"

Ah, if only a person could make a living pleasing just one partner, then I wouldn't have to return to work. I didn't think Christine wanted me to respond to her comment because that would require removing my mouth from her clit.

She'd automatically opened her legs wider for me, and I was using both my mouth and fingers. As I moved through her wetness, I continued to open her up. I'd managed to prominently display the sensitive bud allowing me to suck gently. Almost as though it was a natural progression, I moved the tip of my index finger to the very edge of her opening. I teased along the outside but didn't go inside. I was waiting for her to tell me that's what she wanted. I got my wish after a few seconds.

"Yes, go inside." She was panting now.

One finger slid inside, and I curled it slightly to reach the spongy surface where I knew I'd find her g-spot. I continued to lick and suck as I added to her pleasure with my finger.

Her moans increased in volume until I heard her cry out my name and felt the pulse of her vagina against my fingers. The tiny contractions after the big event kept coming for what seemed like minutes but were probably only seconds.

I kissed my way up her body and marveled at her satisfied smile. "I haven't felt this good in years. Thank you," she said.

"Oh, believe me, it was my pleasure, and I hope it will be my pleasure several more times this morning."

Christine turned me to my side and began her assault on my body. Soon, I was writhing in pleasure and calling out to her. I hoped she liked a vocal lover because I was never one to hold back.

It was three hours and multiple orgasms later before we emerged from the cabin to make our way to the showers. This was a weekend I would never forget. The only other occasion I'd ever spent this much time in bed with a new lover was my first experience with a woman. It was so fresh and wonderful, I couldn't get enough. It seems like I couldn't get enough again. I felt like a teenager instead of a middle-aged woman. I was grateful I hadn't lost my desire for sex. It was going to be fun now that I was a lot more experienced.

CHAPTER TWENTY-THREE

Colette

Daria brought a friend with her to Bumbershoot. She was an attractive butch. Not necessarily my type, because I tended to go for more feminine-looking women, like Serena or Melissa.

I didn't know if my sister was interested in Jo. I hoped she wasn't because Jo was flirting shamelessly with me all day long. I didn't want to be rude, so I suppose I never rebuffed her overtures. She offered to help me move the heavier items from Melissa's place. My sister had given her a brief background. I wasn't sure if that was what I wanted at this point. My love life was in a shamble, and I was a little confused about how I felt at this moment.

Maybe I could see if Melissa and I should give it another go. We were together for eight years. Perhaps that meant something.

"I heard you have a motorcycle. That's cool. We should go riding sometime," Jo tossed out.

"Sure, that would be fun, but I'm not certain I'm going to keep it."

"You're not?" Daria asked.

"I need money to pay for my last quarter."

"Oh, right. I don't have a lot, but I could help you out a little. Or maybe you could ask Isabella," Daria answered.

Isabella was our oldest sister and second mom to all. Whenever one of us was in trouble, she swooped in to clean up the mess. She'd taken in Andrea's two daughters when Child Protective Services found them living in the woods.

Andrea was the sister a few years older than myself. She struggled with the mental illness that normally skipped a generation, showing up randomly in a person's family tree. I suppose people expect it to emerge in their family, but like Russian roulette, we didn't know who would get the bullet. Andrea did, and the rest of us breathed easier. Although, we felt a lot of guilt when the terrible disease hadn't afflicted the rest of us.

Schizophrenia is a horrific malady. An imaginary Native American man taunted Andrea every day. He whispered in her ear, giving her instructions and messages on what she should do, and where she should go. Since she'd lived most of her teenage years in the woods or as a homeless person on the streets, we'd lost track of her after she ran away from home. I wasn't equipped to care for my nieces, but Isabella was.

Andrea had taken off with the father when she was a teen before we knew about her illness. By the time we realized her living condition, and how she was raising her children, it was almost too late. They were both school age but hadn't attended school. It was a long road for both of them. At least their father made the right decision for his kids when he contacted Daria to come get them. He was done with my sister and her illness and had decided fatherhood wasn't for him.

Andrea would call me every once in a while, begging me to take her away from the group home. I visited her, but not very often. She was better off in the home, and everyone in my family knew it.

"Isabella has enough on her plate," I answered.

"Yeah, I suppose you're right about that."

"You can always ride on the back of my bike. Anytime you want," Jo offered with a smile on her face.

I didn't answer. Somehow, I couldn't see myself riding bitch in the back as Jo made lazy circles along with the other Dykes on Bikes at the pride parade in Seattle.

She was a nice enough person. As the day progressed, I'd agreed to take her with me to the island to meet Red and Blackie. The several drinks I'd had throughout the day as we wove in and out of the small venues, certainly helped to lubricate my interest.

†

My head was pounding the next morning when Jo showed up to my place in Seattle. She was entirely too chipper for me, and after I grabbed my bag, I asked if she would drive to the nearest coffee shop.

"Sure thing, beautiful lady."

I cringed. I definitely gave off the wrong signals yesterday. Whenever I played music, it was all part of the show—to flirt a little with the audience. I guess the flirting sometimes spilled over into other parts of my life.

Jo had a stereotypical monster truck and helped my five-foot frame into the cabin like the chivalrous butch she was. I gave her points for avoiding my ass.

The conversations we had yesterday were a bit fuzzy, so I reopened the small talk door by asking her about herself. "Sorry, I forgot what you do for a living."

"Construction. I'm a carpenter."

It fit. "I guess the housing business is feast or famine, huh?"

"Sometimes, but Seattle is a safe market, or in the surrounding areas. I haven't had any trouble finding work. I've got everything I need, except a beautiful lady by my side. I've been single now for three years. Sorry about your breakup. That's tough. Eight years is a long time."

I was racking my brain trying to remember what I'd told her about Melissa. Did Jo think she dumped me? I took the safe route and mumbled, "Yeah, it is."

After that, we didn't talk about too much until we reached the island.

†

Flipping up the latch on the gate Melissa had installed with my help, I let myself and Jo into the backyard. Red and Blackie came running, tongues flapping against their jaws. Red's tail was swinging back and forth excitedly.

I got down on my knees and wrapped my arms around his neck and kissed his nose. He was such a sweet dog. After I released Red, I stroked Blackie's silky fur and pecked his snout.

"Beautiful dogs," Jo remarked.

"Have you guys been good for Aunt Candie?" I started to walk around to the sliding glass door and the back deck. I wasn't sure if Candie was home or not. The answer to my question appeared when the sliding glass door opened, and Candie emerged wearing shorts and a tank top. She narrowed her eyes at us. "Hey, I didn't think you would be by this early."

"Candie, this is Jo. She offered to drive me here."

Jo stuck out her hand, which Candie promptly ignored, responding with a curt nod. "Are you going to take them to the beach?"

"Yeah. Do you wanna come?" I asked.

She shook her head. "Any idea how long you plan on keeping them here?"

Jo was looking back and forth between Candie and me. She seemed to pick up on the strained interchange but mercifully kept quiet. There was no doubt whose side Candie was on, like the rest of our friends. I was the evil bitch who dumped Melissa.

"I was hoping you would be able to look after them until I finish my last quarter of school. After that, I can get a full-time job and find a place where I'll be able to keep them. Is that a problem for you or Melissa?"

"I'm not doing this for you. I'm doing it for Melissa," Candie responded. "Just make sure you don't take advantage of her any more than you already have." She turned back around and went into the house.

"What was that about?" Jo asked.

"Seems everyone has taken sides, and I appear to be the only one to blame in our breakup."

"A failed relationship is never one-sided."

"Tell that to our group of friends."

"Fuck 'em. They aren't your friends if they can't find a way to see all perspectives."

"The truth is that Melissa is a genuinely nice person. Finding many faults with her is hard. She doesn't allow emotion to slip out, but apparently, the breakup finally caused a crack in her stoic exterior. I am responsible for that crack. That's a fact."

"If the relationship were so solid, you'd still be together. Sometimes, shit happens, and it's all for the best in the long run. It doesn't have to be one person's fault; it could just mean you two weren't meant to be. People fall out of love all the time."

"I'd rather not talk about this anymore. Playing with the dogs is the kind of therapy I need right now."

"Okay. Sure. Sure. Whatever you need."

Damn, I was traveling down that path again. I could tell Jo was a genuinely nice person who I would undoubtedly disappoint. I was falling into a familiar pattern—hooking up with a person who would take care of me and then tossing them aside when they didn't suit me any longer. At least that's what everyone would believe.

†

After we deposited the dogs in the backyard, I knocked on the sliding glass door. Candie reluctantly opened the door and waved us in. I'm not sure what possessed me, but like those people who rubberneck at fatal car crashes, I had to ask, "So, is Melissa in Victoria this weekend with Tori and Janet?"

"Yeah." The answer from Candie was curt.

"Um, I guess she didn't ask you or anyone else to go with her, huh?"

"Not that it's any of your business, but I went up there for her birthday so she wouldn't be alone, but we're not dating or anything so why would she ask me to go."

"You'd like to," I muttered under my breath.

"What?"

"Nothing. So, she's not seeing anyone?" I asked.

"Why the twenty questions?"

"Just because we broke up doesn't mean I don't want her to be happy and move on."

I believed what I was saying, and there was a big part of me that truly wanted her to be happy. I had to assuage my guilt somehow, but if I was honest with myself, I wanted to know if she'd found someone new. There was a tiny part of me that wondered if I'd made the biggest mistake of my life throwing our relationship away like yesterday's garbage.

"Yeah, right. Sorry I don't know anything other than she'll be back by to pick up Sarasota and Freud before returning to cowpoke land."

"The cats are here? Can I see them?"

"Be my guest. They're in the master bedroom napping."

Jo dutifully followed me into the room that brought back memories. For the most part, those memories were good. We spent a lot of time in the master bedroom because it was so large and had a good-sized TV nestled into an oak entertainment center. We would snuggle together and watch American Idol. Both of us were big Kelly Clarkson fans. Melissa loved it when I would rub her head until she fell asleep. The king-sized bed offered plenty of room for us and the cats. Melissa didn't allow the dogs on the bed, which I understood. Red was nearly a hundred and twenty pounds, and Blackie at least sixty.

I blinked away the memories and sat on the edge of the bed petting both Sarasota and Freud. Even though I was more of a dog person, the cats were special. They never acted like cats. Sarasota was as close to a dog as any canine I'd ever had. She'd greet us both at the door whenever we came home.

They were both purring, and I missed seeing them. I realized that back at my place in Seattle, I was all alone now. It was somewhat disconcerting. I'd been so distracted by school and Serena to notice. I missed having animals in my life. It was going to be a long, hard, quarter before I could unite full-time with my dogs.

I kissed them both on the nose while wiping a tear that had escaped. I'd made my bed, and it wasn't here on the island, so I needed to run from this room before I started crying in front of Jo.

"I'm not really a cat person, but I suppose they're pretty."

"Come on, let's go."

"I'll take you out to eat. You must be hungry by now."

"Thanks, I am. Let's go to Coupeville. They have some nice places that are better than Oak Harbor. Then we can catch the ferry and head back to Seattle."

Jo grabbed my hand and pulled me from the bed. Not releasing her hold, I let her lead me out, hand in hand. Candie was scowling in the foyer as we walked out the front door. Tough. Let her report back to Melissa and the rest of the gang.

CHAPTER TWENTY-FOUR

Sarasota

I didn't mind when Melissa dropped us off with Candie. I liked taking naps on the big bed. That was where I was when Colette sat down on the edge and woke me up.

A strange woman was standing awkwardly by her side, and if I hadn't been peacefully sleeping, I would have mustered a bit of energy to hiss at her. Not that I normally hissed at strange women, but this one had to go and make that backward compliment. She didn't have to say she was a dog person right in front of us. She should have known that cats require worshiping from all humans.

I knew I should have been mad at Colette, but she was showing Freud and me the right amount of attention, and I enjoyed having her pet my head and run her hands down my back. She even kissed my nose, and that's when I noticed her tear. Maybe she was missing Melissa or us. I wasn't sure if that was a good thing or not, and I couldn't ask Freud about it. He was kinda dumb about those things. My brother was a pretty package, and very sweet, but dumb as rocks.

I was the one who figured out an escape route when Melissa took us to the vet for them to do unspeakable things. I only forgave her because she always cut up little treats for us. It took several servings for me to cave. Freud, the dumb ass, forgave her right away. He was so happy to see her that all it took was her saying, "Oh, my pretty babies, I'm so sorry, but I don't want to turn you two into a breeding factory, and I can't worry that you'll escape and get yourselves in trouble."

As if I would stick my butt in the air for just any old cat. I preferred rubbing up against big bear. He was the softest stuffed animal I'd ever cozied up to. I didn't need no stinkin' tomcat to take care of my needs. Anyway, that was old news, and I had eventually forgiven Melissa.

I narrowed my eyes when I saw that doofus she was with grab her hand. I didn't like that one bit, not one bit at all. Jumping off the bed, I followed them. Candie was leaning against the wall giving them both the evil eye. Good for you, Candie. I don't like her either.

After the door closed, I followed Candie back into the living room where she was watching a movie or something. She sat down, and I decided I'd let her smother me with attention while she watched her show, so I curled up in her lap and lifted my chin for her to scratch.

"Meow," I exclaimed. Letting her know she should continue.

"Yeah, Sarasota, you're a pretty girl." She kept petting me.

Damn right I am. I began purring. Humans liked that when cats purred.

CHAPTER TWENTY-FIVE

Melissa

Even though the weekend went way too fast, I was happy we left relatively early on Monday. I didn't want to get home too late since I had to work the next day. The logistics of picking up my cats and taking Christine to her car were complicated but not difficult. Kenmore Air was sort of on the way home.

Neither one of us were fans of fast food, but we didn't want to leave the cats in the car while we shared a meal. I suggested we grab something at the deli on the way home and that seemed to be all right with Christine.

My enamored feelings for Christine were growing, but I didn't want to make the same mistakes I had made in past relationships. It was way too soon for the *L* word, but I had to admit we were traveling down that track and fast.

When we got to her car in the parking lot of Kenmore Air, I don't think either one of us wanted the weekend to end. I reluctantly got out of my car and stood next to the driver's side with her as she leaned on her Isuzu.

"I wish you didn't live so far away. Do you have plans next weekend?" I asked.

She smiled. "I think I'm coming to visit you. I'll pack a bag and leave from Children's. I'll take Sasha to my friend's house the night before. Unless you have plans."

I put my arms around her and squeezed. "I suppose I can hang on for four days," I whispered in her ear.

"Don't be scared, but I'm pretty sure I'm falling in love with you, Melissa."

I didn't want to be afraid, but I was, just a little. Things always started out this way. The other person confessing their love and then five or even eight years later, it was *hasta la vista*, baby. I didn't think I had it in me again to survive another breakup. I didn't respond, but I didn't pull away either. I felt her arms relax, and I took a step away.

"I better get on the road. I'll see you on Friday. I'll cook dinner for us. Just let me know an approximate time when you'll be there."

Shit, I felt like I was making the arrangements for a business deal. Christine's sad look was all it took to shake free the emotion I was holding in. I caressed her face.

"Ditto." It had to be enough for now because that was all I had.

†

I immersed myself into work and tried not to think too much about my conflicting feelings. Fear was certainly at the forefront, but love was making its move in the outer lane and gaining fast. Christine continued to call me late at night, and I was existing on fumes and coffee because sleep was still dancing just outside my reach.

It was somewhat anticlimactic when I told her on the phone in words other than *ditto* that I was fairly sure I was falling in love with her as well. I could hear the smile in her voice on the other end.

"Breathe, Melissa. It will all be okay. The universe always provides whatever we need."

"I know you're probably an old soul or something and much further along the path than I am. I respect that, but you should know I'm not very spiritual. It's one of the many reasons Colette and I split. I have deep emotions and thoughts, but spirituality seems to evade me. I'm not sure I even know what spirituality means. It is such a foreign concept. So far, for me, love has been evasive and a liar. It causes a great deal of hesitation." I sighed.

She laughed. "You're probably more spiritual than you think. Sometimes the wisest action we can take is the one that appears most bizarre and least practical to everyone around us. And yet we often feel as if all our choices are defined by what others expect. There is wisdom is listening to our hearts and opening ourselves up to surprise and the magic and mystery of life."

I suppose if I was someone who believed in reincarnation, this was the point in my life where I was probably supposed to learn a valuable lesson. I didn't realize the lectures and teachings were still on the horizon.

†

I was zoning off as I drove home on Thursday evening, which was probably not a good thing. Since I wasn't paying attention when I turned onto my street and traveled to the end of the road, I hadn't noticed Colette sitting on my front stairs until I pulled into the driveway.

After turning off the car, I sat for a few seconds, willing my heart to stop beating so hard.

"Hi," she greeted.

"What are you doing here?" I asked softly. There was a kind of resignation in my voice. I'd lost my previous anger and thought I'd made it to a place of acceptance, but the worms in my stomach told a different story.

"I'm feeling a little lost right now."

Setting my bag down, I sat next to her. "What's going on?"

"Serena and I split up. She told me I was too needy. Am I?"

I didn't know how to answer her. I shrugged. "You're sensitive. An artist. I don't know. I guess you have deep emotions and you like to explore them a lot. You were always more vocal about your feelings than me, and I suppose I never quite knew how to fix it when you got sad or discouraged."

"I didn't want you to fix me, Melissa. I wanted you to listen."

"I know. I suppose I get uncomfortable with negative emotions. I always have been one to believe I could choose my attitude and not let sadness rule. Karma is a bitch, you

173

know? It was a bitter pill to know a person can't always remain in control of their emotions, no matter what some inspirational speaker says. I get it now. I still don't want negative emotions to define me, but there isn't anything wrong with letting those feelings surface now and again."

"I heard a rumor…"

I raised my eyebrow. "A rumor?"

"I heard you're dating a scientist. Is it true?"

"Yeah."

"Serious?"

I nodded. "I think maybe it is or it could be if I don't fuck it up."

"I don't suppose…."

"Trust is a hard thing to rebuild."

"I'm sorry. I know I was the one who fucked things up, not you."

"No matter what anyone says, Colette, when two people split, it is never just one person's fault. I-I wanted a chance to figure out what part I played and try to make it better, but I needed you to meet me halfway…"

"I know. A decision I'll probably regret for a long time. I should go."

"I do have a guest bedroom. You can stay. I'd rather you not drive if you're upset." I stood and began to walk up the stairs.

"Okay. At least let me make you dinner."

"Um… I don't think you'll find much to make a meal, no matter how creative you get."

Colette's gaze roved up and down my body. "How much weight have you lost?"

I shrugged. "I'm sure I picked up a few pounds over Labor Day weekend. Cooking for one is not a lot of fun."

She followed me into my chalet and opened the refrigerator. Feta cheese, Kalamata olives, and a tomato sat on the shelf. Then she opened my cabinets and found an equally pitiful assortment of food. She shook her head. "God, you're worse than a bachelor."

"There's a decent pizza place. I'll place the order."

"That sounds good because you're right—except for Greek salad, there's not much to work with here."

†

We sat at the dinette set. This was the location of the original crime. I could almost see the crime scene tape wrapped around my shocked expression. The image made me laugh nervously, like when a person doesn't know how to react to tragedy, so they start to giggle.

She looked up at me with a piece of pizza in her hand. "What?"

"Nothing you want me to elaborate on. I just had a weird visual. You do realize this is where you told me it was over."

Her eyes went wide. "Probably not one of my better moments. I was honestly trying to protect your feelings by not telling you the whole story. I'm a shithead."

"I heard she was beautiful. Young."

"Oh, Melissa, you have to know how gorgeous you are. I didn't leave you for someone more attractive or younger."

I set down the pizza in my hand. I wasn't very hungry anymore. "I shouldn't have dredged that topic up again."

"What's she like?"

175

"Who? Christine?"

"Is that her name, the one you're seeing now?"

I nodded. "She's intelligent, kind, a cyclist, and she doesn't need me to support her." I knew that was a tiny jab and felt bad when Colette cringed. "Sorry, I just meant she has everything on my list."

"Wow, you made a list."

"I did and guess what was near the top?"

"Financially stable?"

"No, that's in the middle somewhere."

"Okay, I'll bite, what's near the top?"

"A serious cyclist."

She laughed. "I did like to bike, just not as much as you. I always thought having your own hobbies or passions was a good thing for couples."

I couldn't help myself, I had to dredge up old wounds. "You know, I should thank you. If it hadn't been for my hurt feelings when you were planning to go to Italy with your cousin and didn't want me to join you, I would have never got online to explore lesbian biking clubs. I did it because I was pissed at you." I laughed. "But then, even after I joined, I wanted you to share in the fun. Couples go on vacation together, not apart. That's how my dad used to screw around on my mother. He would vacation in Florida while we stayed in Baltimore. You had to know that would be salt in an old wound."

"I didn't want to go to Italy without you to have an affair. That never crossed my mind. I was exploring my roots. We have family over there."

"Greece, Italy, they're both locations known for romance. It cut deep hearing you wanted to go without me."

Colette looked down at her plate. "I know."

"I should have known something was drastically wrong then, but like my emotions, I stuffed it under the rug, hoping the dirt wouldn't show. My mother would have apoplexy over that visual."

"Your mom will never forgive me, will she?"

"She doesn't know about Serena, but still, no, she won't. You know what Italian mothers are like with their children."

"Not my Italian mother. I don't think she ever wanted kids. She only did what was expected. Your mom was more nurturing to me than my mother ever was." Colette took a sip of her water.

"Sorry, she knew how hurt I was. She holds grudges. It's the Italian way."

"She was good to me. Maybe someday I can do something to make up for my…"

I picked up my plate and took it to the sink to rinse it off. "I'll go get you a towel and set up the pull-out bed downstairs for you. If you leave the door open, I'm sure Freud or Sarasota will visit you."

"I miss them. I miss a lot of things," she said wistfully.

I let the comment dangle in the air until it disappeared in a puff of smoke. After walking into my master bath and grabbing a towel and one of those extra toothbrushes from the dentist, I handed them to her and walked down the stairs to make up the bed. She dutifully followed and didn't make another comment.

The daylight basement was like a small apartment without a kitchen. The large room had a pull-out sofa, TV and stand, elliptical machine and side table for books or beverages. I grabbed the remote and handed it to Colette.

"You know how it works, in case you want to watch television. Um, I need to make a phone call. You have everything you need?"

"To Christine?"

"Yeah."

"Will she be upset that I'm here?"

"I don't know. I guess I'll find out."

Colette looked a little lost, so I took a few steps forward and gathered her in my arms. We hugged for a long time, and I realized, at this moment, I felt more connected to her than in the entire year before we split. After we broke apart, I kissed her cheek. "Goodnight. If you need me, I'll be upstairs."

The glistening in her eyes nearly broke down my defenses. It would have been so easy to invite her to my bed and comfort her, but I knew if I did that, the consequences of my decision would set my life on a path I wasn't sure I wanted to travel. At least, if I left now, I remained at the fork in the road and could decide which was the better trail.

CHAPTER TWENTY-SIX

Colette

I was still trying to figure out why I'd driven to Cle Elum to cry on Melissa's shoulder. I hadn't full-out cried yet, but I was on the verge. There was hesitation in Melissa's eyes before she left to make her call.

The hug had felt so right, and I almost made a move, but hadn't I done enough already? I wasn't sure whatever I'd broken either of us could fix. Glue and duct tape wasn't the answer, and that's what it felt like it would be if we slept together. I was lonely, and she was the fix-it girl so she would have gone along to remove the sadness.

I needed perspective, so I called my sister.

"Hello," Daria answered.

"Hey. I need some advice."

"Okay."

"I'm in Cle Elum at Melissa's…"

"Oh, Colette. Tread carefully."

"I know."

"Have you considered what you really want? If you want to make a go of it with Melissa, you have to be willing to explore everything that went wrong and find a therapist that both of you can see. A person that won't be aligned with one of you. You're my sister, and I love you, but it wasn't fair to have Melissa go to couples counseling with your therapist. I had to agree with her. I think she was justified in feeling he was more sympathetic to how you were feeling."

"She told you that?"

"We talked, yes. I liked Melissa. I thought she was good for you, but if you didn't or don't think so, you need to let her go. Don't hang on because it's the easier road to travel."

"I don't know what I want. I made a mistake, but I'm not sure the ultimate outcome wasn't inevitable."

"Getting together with someone is the easy part, staying with them takes work no matter who you choose. Take some time to figure out what you want and need in a relationship and then you can determine if the two of you can make a go of it."

"She met someone."

Daria paused before answering. "Oh. Is it serious?"

"It sounded like it could be. I want her to be happy, so maybe I need to walk away and let her explore this without my influence."

"I can't believe I'm going to say this because it is so cliché, but if you love something, let it go, and if it comes back, it was meant to be. Colette, you already answered your own question. You don't need my advice. You already know what to do. I'm glad you're thinking of what's best for her. That's the sister I know and love."

"Thanks, Daria. I love you."

"You're welcome. Let's do something this weekend unless you have other plans. Jo was very enamored with you. She keeps asking me if she has a chance. Tread lightly there as well. She's a good friend. If there's a spark there, that's fine, but don't start something with her because you feel alone. That won't help."

"I know. I need to be clear with her that friendship is the only thing on the table right now."

"Good. Call me tomorrow and let me know what's up."

"All right. Bye."

"Talk to you later."

†

I propped the pillows behind the bed and flipped on the TV. I began to channel surf in an attempt to distract me from thinking too much about my life. Out of the corner of my eye, I saw Sarasota and Freud cautiously pad down the stairs.

Sarasota sat down and began licking her paw. I laughed because I imagined her acting cool and aloof. Freud jumped on the bed and rolled over showing me his belly.

I started to rub Freud's belly, and Sarasota took a few steps closer. Her blue eyes looked at me warily. I turned my attention back to the cat who welcomed my attention.

"Hi there, handsome. I've missed you guys." I glanced at Sarasota. "You too, little princess."

I guess my last comment worked on Sarasota because she jumped up on the bed and let me pet her.

"How's your mom doing?" I asked.

Sarasota lifted her head, and if I didn't know any better, I would have thought she gave me the evil eye. Her purring stopped, but she didn't move away.

"I know you probably think I'm the scum of the earth. Well, get in line, because I share that opinion. I do care even though my actions don't exactly match my sentiments. I'm trying to figure it out. I promise I won't do anything more to hurt her."

That must have been the right thing to say because Freud licked my hand and Sarasota resumed her purring.

I couldn't hear what Melissa was saying, but I heard her muffled voice above me. I kept the television on low, not because I wanted to eavesdrop, but more out of respect for disturbing her peace.

The cats must have come down to visit because she was on the phone, but it was clear where their loyalties remained. I heard the water run and figured she was now in bed after finishing her phone call. Both Sarasota and Freud jumped off my bed and made their way back upstairs. I guessed they were hanging out with me until she finished her call.

I was all alone now. I needed a flash of clarity because my thoughts remained jumbled. It was like I was in a fog and couldn't see one foot in front of me. The future was far from clear. What did I really want? That was the million-dollar question.

CHAPTER TWENTY-SEVEN

Sarasota

Melissa was pacing after she came back upstairs, and then she grabbed her cell phone. I could tell she was nervous. Normally, I would stick by her while she was on the phone, especially when she was smiling, but tonight, her smile was gone.

I swished my tail and started to go downstairs. I didn't trust Colette. She was the reason why Melissa lost her smile. I was going to keep my eye on her and report back to Melissa. I could be a double agent. If I found out something I didn't like, I'd bite Colette right in front of Melissa, and that would be an obvious enough message to get my point across. Pun intended.

I sat down on the rug at a respectable distance and trilled at my joke. Humans didn't understand what it meant when cats trilled, but it was our version of a human chuckle.

Freud followed me, like the loyal brother he was. He ignored my trill, not even asking what had prompted the response, and made a beeline for the bed. He was a lot more forgiving than I was. His complete trust in humans was baffling to me. Sure, I was more affectionate than the average cat, but at least I knew how to hold back on occasion.

I was nonchalantly cleaning my paw when she confessed that she missed us. Well, of course she did. I decided to play along and jumped on the bed to receive my fair share of adulation. I threw in a mellow purr to put her off her game, but when she asked how Melissa was doing, my hackles went up. I gave her my most disapproving look.

At least she admitted she was a schmuck. I guess there was true remorse in her voice, so I stayed for a little while longer until I heard the sounds of Melissa getting ready to go to bed. Freud's ears perked up as well. He waited for me to make a move first, but I knew he was going to leave soon. Freud was a comfort hog, and Melissa's mattress was a lot more comfortable to sleep on than the pull-out bed. I thought it fitting that Colette would have to sleep on the less comfy bed. Served her right for making Melissa cry.

Melissa was staring at her ceiling when Freud and I settled into our normal spots on the bed. She was absently petting us when she sighed.

"Damn. Just when I was starting to get my life back on solid ground, a small Tsunami with Colette's name on it splashes over me. Do you think I owe it to her to see if things can be repaired or should I follow my heart and go for it with Christine? I feel like I have one foot in each world."

"Meow," I responded and hoped she understood. I wanted to communicate to her that this was something only she could answer. No one else should tell her what was the right thing to do. I knew she was still seeing a therapist. She told her dad that a few days ago. I tried not to let that bother me since I was her primary confidant. I had to admit the other woman had better credentials than me. In my defense, they didn't let cats go to college—at least not a fancy brick and mortar college. But I had an advanced degree from the college of life in reading humans and knowing exactly what they needed. I put my paw on her chest to remind her I was there for her. I inched my way up. Normally, I wouldn't stoop to lick her chin like Freud, but today, I sensed she needed that extra show of affection.

She kissed my nose. "Thanks, Sarasota."

"Meow," I let her know she was most welcome.

CHAPTER TWENTY-EIGHT

Melissa

After I'd set Colette up downstairs, I paced my bedroom for a few minutes. I wasn't exactly sure what I would say to Christine. *Oh, hey, you'll never guess what happened today? Colette dropped by. I invited her over for pizza. She's in the guest bedroom right now. How was your day?*

That sounded absurd in my own head, so I imagined how ridiculous it would play over the phone. I wouldn't blame Christine if she went running for the hills never to call again.

My cats were lounging on the bed, but the minute I grabbed my phone and took a big breath, they ran out of the room. I didn't blame them. This wasn't going to be pretty. What could I possibly say to help Christine understand the level of turmoil I was feeling?

Time to face the music. I pushed the buttons to connect with her. She wouldn't think anything about the call. It was a normal ritual. One of us usually called right about this time of night.

"Hey you." She sounded chipper. Happy.

"Hi." My tone revealed the exact opposite emotion.

She picked up on the tone right away. "What's the matter? You sound like you lost your best friend. Did you have a tough day at work?"

"Colette was sitting on my front stairs when I got home."

"Oh, I see. I suppose you want to cancel this weekend."

"No, no I don't. She was upset. I couldn't turn her away. It's complicated."

"We should probably do this in person."

"Do what in person? What do you think we're doing?"

"Ending things?" she tentatively tossed out.

"That's not what we're doing. I'm being honest with you and telling you something I think is important information. My definition of a lie isn't just answering a question untruthfully; it's being evasive about stuff that is kind of a big deal."

"What makes this a big deal?" she asked with a hitch in her voice.

"I think that's fairly obvious."

"Why come to you? Does she want you back?"

"No, well, maybe, I don't know. Serena dumped her. Told her she was too needy."

"Hmm."

"Hmm what? It sounds like you have an opinion."

"I haven't met her yet to have an opinion, other than she was a fool to dump you, and I'm sorry you're experiencing any pain right now. I suppose I don't like her much because of that."

"Nothing's changed. I still want you to come up this weekend. We'll talk more, and I'll do some soul searching over the next twenty or so hours."

"Don't stay up all night, okay?"

"Sleep is a slippery little sucker lately."

"Call if you change your mind about me coming up tomorrow."

"I won't."

"Really, no pressure, but I have to put this out there. I love you, Melissa. Sweet dreams."

"Sweet dreams to you too. I'll see you tomorrow. We'll talk then."

I shut off my phone and laid my head back closing my eyes for a second. I didn't have a lot of time to sort through my feelings, and it was frustrating. It felt like I was untangling two sets of Christmas lights, and I was tempted to toss them both out and start all over with a new set. I wondered if that was what I was doing. I couldn't make sense of my conflicting feelings with Colette, so the easy decision was to obtain a brand-new love life. I tugged at that string a little more and extended the analogy. But what if the old lights didn't work anymore? Didn't my Christmas tree deserve new lights?

Sarasota interrupted my thoughts when she jumped up on the bed, and then I started talking about Tsunamis of all things. Sometimes, Sarasota would look at me like she understood every word I was saying. It was ridiculous, I know, but that didn't stop me from using her as my sounding board.

†

After tossing and turning most of the night, I woke up at about five o'clock to the smell of coffee. I'd fallen asleep not even an hour earlier, but since I was usually at my office by six-thirty, I hoisted my tired body out of bed seeking the liquid gold.

Rubbing my bleary eyes, I saw Colette sitting at the dinette staring out the window with what I assumed was a cup of coffee sitting in front of her. She turned her head in my direction.

"Good morning, I made coffee. I hope you don't mind."

"Not at all. You're a Goddess." I don't know why I blurted that out. It was like the past three months hadn't happened, and it was perfectly normal for Colette to sit at the table drinking coffee. Although, in my previous universe and not this alternate one, I was typically the first person up in the morning and the one who made the coffee.

"You're up early," I stated the obvious.

"Couldn't sleep," was her cryptic reply.

"Join the parade. Welcome to my world."

Tears glistened in her eyes. "You know the kind, honorable thing to do would be to walk out of your life right now and never come back."

I started fixing my coffee. I needed to occupy myself before responding. My fridge was empty of most items, but I always had a healthy supply of that terrible non-dairy creamer. Every morning after I finished my coffee, the

189

remnants of whatever chemicals were in the nasty stuff remained looking a lot like the bottom of a paint can.

Leaning on the counter and stirring my coffee, I ventured what I thought was a neutral reply. "You know, lesbians are famous for remaining friends after splitting up, so why would you never come back?"

She smiled. "True. I guess I could do a lot worse in the friend category. That Leo in you makes you fiercely loyal. Sometimes to a fault."

The last part of the comment reminded me of how vigorously I had defended Colette to my friends when they'd insisted she was drinking again. I shrugged. "That's what my mom always used to say. She worried I would get caught up in the wrong crowd and do whatever my friends suggested, covering for them and, consequently, getting in deep shit myself. It never happened because I was a good girl, and ultimately, I chose the right path. That is until I became a lesbian," I joked.

"It was a different time when you came out. Your mom just needed some time and a shift in societal views to get used to the idea."

"I suppose. At the time, I didn't think it hurt as much as I guess it did when she said she wished I would have been a whore on the streets instead of gay. But the fact that I still remember the comment twenty years later speaks volumes to its impact."

This conversation reminded me of the fact that Colette knew a lot more about me and my upbringing than Christine. She knew about my tumultuous relationship with my dad and how I'd made peace with my mom who did, in fact, come around. She knew what an absolute ass my father had been in his youth and how I still had issues with that. He hadn't even been married to my mother for one year before he started cheating on her. She showed me the letters from his mistress. I never quite got over that or my insecurities over infidelity. She knew about my past heartbreaks and my coming-out story.

Christine didn't know any of that yet. I hadn't decided if that was a good or bad thing. The naked truth was Colette knew me, really knew me and Christine didn't. Could she be in love with someone she didn't know? My warts hadn't yet had a chance to surface.

"At least she cared enough to be appalled," Colette responded bitterly. "Is it awful of me to say that what I might miss most of all is being a part of your family? Your mom was… well, a lot more of a mother to me than my own mother. I thought I'd made peace with her in the end, but I suppose old wounds never heal."

My mother had been disgusted to hear how Colette's parents kicked her out at eighteen and left her to fend for herself. Colette's parents were moving to California the minute she graduated from high school, and when she excitedly asked where they were moving to, they had offhandedly informed her she wasn't going. They'd finished raising their kids. Colette was eighteen now. Good luck. See ya later.

"Look, I gotta get moving or else I'll be late for work."

Colette raised her eyebrow. "It's barely five."

"I try to arrive at the office by six-thirty. The night shift is still there, and I'm able to visit with them." I took a nervous sip of my coffee. "I like getting to know all the employees, not only the day shift."

"Too bad it would be a disastrous idea to come work for your hospital after I'm done with school. You're a great leader. I bet they love you."

I could feel the heat rise to my face. "Not everyone, I'm sure. It goes with the territory that at some point, you're gonna piss someone off." I set my cup down on the counter and turned toward the master bath. "We can talk more, but maybe not tonight. Christine is coming."

"Oh. That's okay. I have class today anyway."

I paused in the doorway. "I'm glad you're finishing school. It would have been a travesty if you hadn't with only one quarter left. Sorry, I have to jump in the shower now."

She waved at me to go ahead, and she continued her gaze out the window as if something outside the chalet had the answers for her. Maybe when she ferreted those out, she'd clue me in. I needed answers as badly as she did.

Before I left for work that morning, I hugged her goodbye. We didn't make any plans to connect, just left it wide open. Wide open—that's what everything felt like. Unfortunately, having a wound wide open could be a good or bad thing. The open air sometimes let it heal more quickly, and other times, the open air welcomed the germs inside, and the wound began to fester. Time would tell regarding which would happen to me.

†

Lately, I'd been making it a point to leave work at a reasonable hour on Fridays, and it was getting close to quitting time when my cell phone rang. I absently picked up the phone to look at who might be calling and saw it was

Christine. I was perplexed because she wouldn't normally call me during the day. I wondered if she thought I was on my way out.

"Hello," I answered.

"Hi, Melissa, sorry to call you at work, but I wanted to let you know I got called into work tonight and wondered if it would be okay if I came tomorrow instead?"

She sounded strained, and I suppose my moment of hesitation was enough to fill the empty space.

"I'm still coming. I promise. I can almost feel your worry on the other end of the phone." She attempted to lighten the mood.

"No, no, of course, that's fine. Whenever you can get here will be great," I answered. *Fantastic*, I thought to myself. Now I had another evening to stew and wonder about the complicated mess of feelings stirring around in my stomach. I'd inherited a tendency for ulcers from my mother, and stress always seemed to land squarely in my abdomen. Swallowing your emotions was not a very healthy way to deal with things, but it was definitely an inherited trait.

"Melissa, my feelings haven't shifted in one night. I do have to work. Maybe this is a good thing. It will give you another night to yourself to puzzle through how you're feeling."

"I know." I shifted in my office chair. "Do you have an ETA for tomorrow?"

"I should be able to make it by noon. We can go have lunch and maybe take a walk on that path by your house."

"You mean the Coal Mines Trail or the John Wayne Trail?"

"I don't know. The one you told me we could walk to where you used to take the dogs."

"Oh, the Coal Mines Trail. Yeah, that's a nice path. It's very pretty, and it's still warm enough. I'll get something for a picnic lunch. How does that sound?"

"That sounds wonderful. A picnic lunch in the woods with a beautiful woman is pretty much nirvana to me." Her voice eased into that relaxed quality I'd come to appreciate.

"Thanks for calling. I'll see you tomorrow."

I leaned back in my chair and turned to my computer. I might as well stay a little longer and get some work done on the database. There wasn't any need to rush home now.

CHAPTER TWENTY-NINE

Colette

My dresser, which Melissa had pushed up against the wall in the small living room of her chalet, was a blinding reminder I still had a presence in the house, but I was a hair's breadth away from eliminating all traces of our doomed relationship. She'd been incredibly patient with me and hadn't mentioned anything about removing the large piece of furniture that had to be a constant reminder of the deep fissure. I tried to ignore looking at it and kept my focus on the window and the beauty outside versus the ugliness of the symbol of failure inside.

I should have left much earlier than I did because I hit rush hour traffic heading into Seattle. After Melissa left for work, I stayed a little longer hanging out with the cats. The pace in Cle Elum was a lot like the island, and I missed it. There were many things I liked about living in Seattle, but

I'd become used to the slower pace when I lived on the island with Melissa before I started my schooling and had to rent a room in Seattle.

I would barely make it to class at this rate, and my level of aggravation was increasing by the minute. At least the bumper to bumper cars were a distraction to my soul searching regarding my failed relationship.

I'd noticed the two missed calls from Jo, but I hadn't bothered to listen to the message yet. I wasn't progressing much on I-90 as I tapped my fingers on the steering wheel. I figured I had plenty of time while I waited for the cars to move, so I picked up my phone and listened to the voice mail.

"Hey, just wondering how you were doing? Let me know when you need help to move your furniture. Or maybe we could get together this weekend and take a ride, see a movie, whatever you want." Her message sounded hopeful.

Crappy, confused, I answered the first question. I wasn't sure if I said that out loud, but I definitely thought it.

I wondered how long I could keep my dresser at Melissa's house. I didn't have anywhere to put it, especially since where I was renting had a nasty set of narrow steps leading into my room. I wouldn't be able to contribute the muscle to maneuver those stairs, even with the help of a big strong butch like Jo. Where would I put the monstrosity? I was going back over my decision to take this sentimental piece of furniture from my mother's condo after she passed.

It was rude not to call Jo back right away, but I didn't have answers to any of her questions. How could I wiggle out of this conundrum I found myself in?

†

After class, I sat outside for a minute soaking up the rare sunshine. I could feel the hint of fall in the air. Fall was my favorite season, the colors, the crispness, the mark of something coming to an end that needed to go. I thought back on one of my favorite books, *The Fall of Freddie the Leaf*. It was a brilliant story that helped children all over the world understand loss. Spring or rebirth only occurred after the fall and winter where the leaves and blossoms had to die to make room for new growth.

I wondered if this was how I was supposed to view my relationship. Was I like Freddie, hanging onto the tree, shivering in the cold and trying to avoid the inevitable? Or had I injected an infestation into the relationship I could kill with a pesticide? I shuddered. Maybe I should consider another more natural method. I was generally opposed to pesticides.

I couldn't delay the inevitable anymore. Plucking my phone from my bag, I called Jo.

"Hey, I'm glad you called. I was worried."

Damn, another incredibly sweet woman who I was about to blow off.

"That's sweet. No, I've been in class all day and didn't notice your messages until now." A tiny white lie.

"Oh. So are you up for doing something this weekend?"

The refusal was on the tip of my tongue, but I couldn't make it come out. "Sure, why not? A movie sounds good."

"You probably wouldn't want to see *Resident Evil: Apocalypse*, would you? We could go to *Vanity Fair*, that's a chick flick…"

"Nah, *Resident Evil* is fine. I'm not in the mood for a historical romance."

"Okay, I'll check the times and pick you up." I could hear the excitement in her voice. I felt a little bad for leading her on, but maybe I could navigate this carefully. Saying I was still reeling from the breakup of an eight-year relationship would make sense as to why I didn't want to jump into a new one right away. Friends, we could be friends, I rationalized. Considering all the mutual friends with Melissa were clearly out of the question. Everyone was still pissed at me. I wondered how long that would last.

†

The next day, Jo came to my door. She'd spruced up and wore a crisply ironed Oxford tucked neatly into a pair of Levi's. The wide black belt and shiny motorcycle boots completed the outfit. Her short blonde hair contained a large amount of gel so that it spiked perfectly on her head. Of course, she was wearing some kind of men's cologne. The scent wasn't unappealing, just not what I was accustomed to. Melissa didn't wear perfume but always had a clean, fresh scent. I preferred that to the musky aroma invading my nostrils. I decided it was a bit overpowering for my taste.

She ran around to the passenger side of her monster truck and helped me inside again. This time, I might have felt the brush of her hand against my backside, dangerously close to my ass. Not good. She clearly saw this as a date. I'd have to set her straight… well, not straight exactly, as I remembered that old joke, never straight only forward. But I would have to make it clear where I stood.

"So what's new?" she asked.

Now was as good a time as any. "I went to see Melissa on Thursday and stayed the night."

Her smile turned upside down. I let the confession dangle until it was too uncomfortable for me. I clarified, "Nothing happened. She's seeing someone now."

"Why did you go?"

I shrugged. That was a good question. "I don't know. She's a comfortable place to land when I'm feeling sad. We were friends before we were lovers." This wasn't going exactly as planned. Now she would think when I gave her the friend speech that we might evolve to lovers.

"You could have called me if you needed to talk."

"I don't know you that well."

"Yet. I'm a good listener and have a big shoulder. It's available to you at any time."

I sighed. This was going to be harder than I thought. "You know I can't even consider jumping into something new, right? I've already made enough of a mess of my life. I can't continue on this destructive path. Friendship, that's all I have to offer." There, I'd said it. The ball was in her court now, and I was hoping she wouldn't send a perfect lob back in my direction leaving open the possibility of more. I didn't get my wish.

"Friendship is fine with me. The best relationships always begin as solid friendships. I'm a very loyal friend."

"I'm sure you are." Probably as loyal as Melissa.

CHAPTER THIRTY

Melissa

I was up early on Saturday morning, so I took my bike out to clear my head a little. Going for a ride was therapy for me in many ways. I chuckled to myself as I thought maybe that's where my spirituality coalesced. Riding always produced enough endorphins to create an almost out-of-body experience, especially if I combined my exertion with deep thoughts.

I should have brought more water, or at least an energy bar or two because before I knew it, I was fifteen miles from home. A thirty-mile ride might not seem like a lot, but if a person was hauling ass like I was, they could burn five hundred calories in an hour. I turned around realizing my foolishness and hoped I wouldn't hit a wall before I arrived back at my place.

My mind wandered as the pedals went around and around. I wondered if I kept choosing partners who were a lot like my father. He was charming but never very faithful. With each rotation, things were becoming clearer. I didn't want to re-establish my relationship with Colette, no matter how many years we were together. As sure as I knew I was a lesbian, I knew she'd break my trust again. I wanted to rip to shreds the pattern I'd established with my previous relationships. Christine was perfect for me if I could let myself break away from my self-imposed obligations to do everything in my power to make things work. I'd never made commitments lightly, but didn't I deserve to be happy and in a committed, healthy relationship with someone mature enough to work through the hard times?

"I do," I yelled.

I was glad it had taken Colette several months to come back around because if she'd come to my doorstep a month ago, we'd probably be back together.

I must have powered myself home on the promise of a bright future with Christine. A vision of us sitting in rocking chairs with a tuft of silver hair on both our heads, danced in front of me.

After I put my bike away, I ran up the stairs and then tossed a piece of pizza in the microwave before I passed out from an empty stomach and over two hours of hard riding. It was after ten, and I had a bounce in my step as I pulled my sweaty clothes off my body and tossed them in the hamper.

The microwave dinged, and I blew on the slice before taking a big bite. I turned on the shower and then I ripped away another morsel while waiting for the water to warm up.

I had plenty of time to get ready, go to the store, and prepare a picnic lunch. I felt like a weight had lifted from my shoulders as I scrubbed my scalp and started singing off key in the shower.

The solo grocery store in Cle Elum was overpriced, but they made a decent deli sandwich. I had the clerk make me a Turkey on wheat, and for Christine, I remembered she liked rare roast beef. I wasn't sure on the condiments, so I took a guess. Mayonnaise and tomatoes seemed a safe bet. I was sure I could rustle up mustard if she wanted to add that to the sandwich. I had a few condiments in the fridge along with my tomatoes, olives, and feta.

They didn't have quite the selection of cheeses the specialty natural markets Christine frequented always stocked, but I picked up a few varieties, along with some apples, grapes, and strawberries. On a whim, because grocery markets always had those impulse purchase displays, I grabbed several varieties of chips. I later learned she was a plain potato chip kind of gal but was polite enough to eat the honey Dijon I'd picked out over the sour cream and onion.

It was close to noon when I finally walked outside and sat on my stairs waiting for Christine to arrive after putting the sandwiches, cheese, and fruit in my refrigerator. I lifted my face to the sun and was enjoying the warmth with my eyes closed when I heard a car approach. She was right on time. I liked that about her.

A pet peeve of mine was when people arrived late. I thought it was disrespectful of a person's time. The message was, *you aren't as important as me.* Later, I learned that Christine could dawdle quite a bit when there wasn't a specific time we had to be somewhere. I called her a *pokus maximus* during those times. I smiled at her and stood when I heard the car door shut. She hesitated for a fraction before meeting me on the front lawn. I opened my arms up, and she stepped inside. The neighbors be damned. I kissed her in front of a God I didn't believe in, and everyone else.

"What a beautiful day for a picnic. Hang on for a second." She walked back to her car and retrieved her bag and a bouquet.

As soon as she came close, I caught a whiff of the sweet scent. "Wow, those are really fragrant."

"Asian lilies."

"I like these better than roses."

She smiled. "I hoped you would."

The lilies would remain my favorite flower, one she would bring home often.

"You're full of surprises. I like that you always bring me something that smells nice, like the lavender from your garden. Are these from your garden?"

She shook her head. "No, it's too late in the season. Mine have already been harvested."

I tilted my head. "Harvested? It sounds like you were gathering fruit."

She laughed. "Maybe I was. The fruit of love. Did it work?"

I impulsively kissed her again. "It sure did."

I led her into the house so she could drop off her bag and I could put the flowers in water. While I was scrounging around in my cabinets, out of the corner of my eye, I caught her looking around. I pointed to the room off to the right of the main living area. "You can put your bag in there. That's the master bedroom. I know the place is small, but it suits my needs. I don't require a lot of space."

"It's cozy."

I laughed. "That's what all the real estate ads say when they want to describe a tiny house. There's more. It's about 1,500 square feet. I have a daylight basement that is relatively large."

"Sorry, I didn't mean to offend you. I really did mean it's cozy, and that's not at all a bad thing. I like cozy."

She went into the bedroom while I was putting the flowers in a vase I'd found. I assumed she set the bag either on the bed or on the floor since she returned empty-handed.

"Let me give you the two-dollar tour, and then we can grab the food and head out. I don't have a picnic basket, but I suppose a small collapsible cooler should suffice."

"Is that the lesbian version of a tour, like queer as a two-dollar bill? I thought it was a nickel or fifty cent tour."

"Come on. Haven't you heard about inflation?"

"Ah, inflation. Nice concept." She grabbed me and pulled me close. Her passionate kiss had me off-stride for a second. "I'm instituting my own inflation. Those two short kisses weren't nearly enough payment."

"What do I owe you payment for?" I asked.

She wiggled her eyebrows. "For what I plan on doing to you later. I'll expect more kisses as remuneration. This was simply a down payment."

I felt my face flush. "I'm glad you're in a good mood and haven't let our last conversation affect you."

"I asked the universe for something this morning, and when I'm very specific, it always provides. I have faith."

"You should," I answered.

"I forgot. I also brought cheese and fruit. I have it in a cooler in the back of my car."

"Great minds think alike. I got cheese at the store, but I'm sure yours is much better than my selection. Cle Elum doesn't exactly have gourmet food to choose from."

"We should head out soon, I'm starved. I don't know about you but talking about the cheese and fruit just poked my stomach awake."

"Mine too. I went for a ride this morning and didn't think to eat, so I grabbed a piece of leftover pizza that has long been absorbed into my body."

Christine scrunched up her face. "You should take better care of yourself."

"I know. Sometimes I get involved in something and forget to eat."

"How can someone forget to eat?"

"It's pretty easy. I'm like an absent-minded professor on occasion. When I get focused, everything else in my world goes away. You should probably run now. It's not one of my better traits. I'm obsessive times ten. It was a huge complaint from Colette."

"Sorry, I don't scare easily."

I wove my fingers into her thick hair and kissed her again. "Partial pre-payment for tonight."

†

"You are so incredibly lucky to have this trail literally in your backyard... well, close anyway," Christine said.

"I know I do love it up here. Close to the mountains and everything, but I miss the island and my friends. I don't know hardly anyone here, and it can be very lonely for a single lesbian."

Christine stopped and tugged me to the bench twenty yards away. We'd been strolling hand in hand down the path. She carried her cooler over her right shoulder, and I had mine slung on my left.

"I had sort of hoped you considered us in a relationship. You have to know I don't just sleep with anyone. I'm already too far into this to back away now unless that's what you need." Her eyes glistened with unshed tears.

Crap. I had realized what I'd said. I turned to her. "I don't know why I just said that. I had a very cleansing ride today and came to the conclusion I don't want to go back with Colette. I do see a future between the two of us, but…"

"I hate the word but, because everything you said before that three-letter word is now negated."

"Shit, I'm not communicating very well, am I? You'd think in my line of work I would be an expert communicator." I took a deep breath. "I want to do this right. I know the distance is a hurdle, but…" I held up my hand. "Let me finish because the second part isn't bad at all, and it does not negate the first. I'm old enough to avoid the traps that typically befall lesbians. When we decide it is the right time to move in with each other, it will be when we're both ready to buy a house together. That's the ultimate commitment to me, and frankly, I haven't made that leap since my first heartbreak. I'm nowhere near ready for that. I can be madly in love with you until then. I hope that's enough for you."

Christine took my hand and placed a gentle kiss on my lips. "As long as we're moving forward together, it's more than enough. Oh, and we're continuing to have great sex, that's a must."

I laughed. "I agree. Smack me if we somehow get caught up in that lesbian bed-death."

"Hmm, I didn't think you were into that?"

"A figure of speech, because you're correct, to each their own, but pain and pleasure are two separate concepts, and I'm not interested in combining them."

"Good, because that's not my cup of tea either."

"Now, I wouldn't exactly say no to a little bondage. Teasing is good."

"Kinky. A little vanilla with a dash of chocolate. I like it."

"I can be adventurous."

"So, what did you pack for lunch? I think I've been incredibly patient."

"You have. Oh crud, I forgot to ask if you like mustard on your roast beef sandwich. I guessed at mayonnaise and tomato, but we'll have to go back to the house if you want mustard. You distracted me before with the whole talk about inflation and payment for future activities."

"Don't worry. I don't require mustard. I'm impressed you remembered I like roast beef."

"On occasion, I pay attention. Certainly, I'm not as observant as you, but I have my moments."

†

We ate our food in relative peace and had a few furry visitors that hovered a safe distance away watching us. I was about to toss a potato chip to the squirrel doing a fine job of begging when Christine shook her head.

"I don't think it's healthy for them. It's bad enough we consume this stuff without getting the wildlife addicted to junk food."

"But he's so cute."

Christine pulled off a corner of her crust and tossed it in front of the tree rat. That's what my father used to call them right before he would shoot them. That little hunting expedition scarred me for life.

"I don't suppose a tiny piece of wheat bread will kill him." Christine grinned.

I offered the rest of the bread on my sandwich after tearing it into small pieces.

"Can you believe my dad used to hunt these cute little guys? When we were younger and didn't have a lot of money, my mother would dip them in eggs and bread crumbs and fry 'em up for dinner." I shuddered. "I can't believe I used to eat squirrel."

"My dad would bring home all kinds of injured animals, including a squirrel once and a skunk another time. My mother always found out and would have a hissy fit. I learned to love nature from my father. He was a gentle soul, so unlike my mother who we called little Hitler. Hungarian sternness."

I brushed my hands together to rid myself of the crumbs and then stood up. "Ready to head back?"

She took my hand, and we strolled down the path.

†

We were sitting on the back deck, and I wasn't sure what to offer her to drink. Normally, I would have bought a nice bottle of wine and offered her a glass. Not that I was a big wine drinker or someone who drank much at all, but that's what a mature woman does when entertaining. Beer wasn't my thing either. If I drank anything at all, it was Mike's Hard Lemonade. I knew she liked green tea, but that seemed like something a person would suggest late at night or maybe in the morning. Water seemed lame, but that was all I had besides a Mike's.

"Um, I don't know what to offer you to drink. You don't seem like a soda kind of person, and I know you don't drink alcohol..."

"Water is good. Hydration is important."

I scrambled to the kitchen to get us both ice water. I wished I had a lemon slice to drop inside the glass and class it up a bit. I pondered the fact I didn't know a lot about Christine, including her preferred beverage. I wanted to know more about her recovery, because even though she'd been clean and sober for twenty years now, the possibility she might fall off the wagon like Colette was, for lack of better terminology, sobering.

I decided to bite the bullet and get that tiny bit of unease out of the way. I handed her the glass of water. "Does it bother you to be around people who drink?"

She squinted as she looked at me. "No, not at all. I don't like to be around drunks, but if you're in a social situation, alcohol is normally present. Why? Do you drink a lot? Something you haven't shared about yourself?" She grinned.

"Um, no, I don't drink a lot, normally. Sure, I had my wild and crazy times in college, but I'm pretty much a teetotaller, and I never drink and drive. It's a hard and fast rule with me. When Colette first stopped drinking, I supported her by never ordering wine or any other drinks. So did Tori and Janet. Although I must say, Tori was relieved when Colette eventually, after about a year, said it didn't bother her, and Tori quickly resumed having wine with her meals."

"You're worried I'll fall off the wagon or resume my cocaine use," she stated with a frown on her face.

"Sorry, I'm that transparent, huh?"

She nodded. "What would you like to know?"

"Tell me what happened to get you to stop?"

"I knew I was heading for an early grave. I was completely out of control. I checked myself into the best inpatient center I could find. I got myself a sponsor. I worked the program, one day at a time, and I can honestly say I have no desire to return to that way of life."

"I can't even imagine what that's like."

"No, you can't. There's a lot of shame around addiction. I don't drink alcohol because I've seen what it does to people with liver conditions, not because I have a problem with alcohol. So, being around alcohol is not a temptation. That was never my drug of choice like I said before."

"Oh, I didn't know that was the reason. I thought you worked with E.Coli. That's not a liver disease, is it?"

"No, it's not, but the hepatology group is just around the corner, and sometimes, I help with their studies. There are a lot of different conditions I find fascinating and terribly sad at the same time."

"I'm glad there are people like you leading those studies."

Christine took my hand. "Addiction comes in many forms and doesn't care about socioeconomic status. It's a disease, like cancer, but unfortunately, most people don't blame the person suffering from cancer on their lack of willpower. I'm not saying addicts shouldn't accept responsibility for their choices, but until you walk in those shoes, it is hard to understand. Just know this, the reason I'm not going to fall off the wagon isn't because I love you and would be afraid to lose you. I won't do it because of how it affects me personally, and that is the best reason to stay true to one's recovery. I stay clean for me."

"Okay, I get it. Addiction is not about me or someone who doesn't love me enough to stop. It was a lesson my therapist tried to teach me. I didn't learn it well. Ultimatums were the only tool in my limited toolbox, and it obviously didn't work."

"I think I'm a safe bet."

"After twenty years, I'm sure you are."

"I'd be more concerned about whatever health issues I could run away from as a result of my previous cocaine use, although I take excellent care of myself now. At least, if I ever have to face something, I have ties to wonderful clinical trials. They're always on the verge of a breakthrough, and I'll have an inside track to the medications that are being trialed."

"That would be good. I had Hepatitis A when I was younger, and I ended up in the hospital for seven days, then I was laid up for three months. There were other complications, but I remember not having a lot of fun that summer. That was the end of my strict vegetarianism. My mother pushed protein and told me, in no uncertain terms, I was eating meat, and that was all there was to it."

Christine laughed. "I'm looking forward to meeting your mother."

"Now that I'm an adult, I have a modified diet that limits my meat intake, and I don't consume anything I deem cute. That means no beef or pork. Chicken and fish are ugly."

"Baby chicks are adorable."

"I don't eat the babies."

"Sounds like rationalization to me." Christine chuckled and then gave me a serious look. "What else do you want to know? It's not good to start a relationship with doubt or questions, especially since I'm a carnivore and that might offend you." She punctuated the last part of her sentence with a smile to let me know she was teasing.

She let go of my hand and pushed her hands through her hair.

"What else do you think I should know?" I asked.

"Ooh, you're a wily one." She pressed her index finger against her lip. "Hmm, well, I've only been in two long-term relationships with women. The first ended after recovery. She was a practicing alcoholic, and I needed to change people, places, and things. She wanted to continue that life, and I didn't. We were together for a long time. It was hard on her when I left."

"And the other?"

"That's the one I wrote you about. We both moved out here so I could go to school. She has family in Maryland she couldn't separate from. She left and took our daughter with her. I'd already spent the proceeds on my house for school and didn't have the financial resources to fight her. We were going to start adoption proceedings, but she kept delaying those. I should have seen it coming." Christine looked away. I sensed she was trying to hold her emotions in.

"If you aren't the biological parent, you have no rights. I try to stay connected, but she moved on and has a new partner. For the first few years, she would let my daughter visit. I treasured those times. That came to an abrupt end a few years ago. I send gifts, money sometimes for guitar lessons and such, but the contact is more and more infrequent every year that passes," she continued.

I took her hand again. "I thought at one time I wanted children, but to be honest, I'm glad I never traveled that road. I'm not very good with kids. They make me nervous. I always want to fix things, and when babies or children start crying, it breaks my heart. Now, at my age, that ship has definitely sailed. My good friends have three little ones, and gosh, I don't know how they have the energy. I like being the cool aunt. That role suits me much better."

"You're probably not giving yourself enough credit. I think you'd make a wonderful mother, but I get it that the role is not for everyone. I guess it works out for us since kids don't seem to be something you'd be interested in."

"That's true unless you count furbabies. I'll always have those." I smiled.

"Something you said before piqued my interest."

This sounded serious, so I made sure to show her the whites of my eyes. "Go on."

"You mentioned something about the ultimate commitment of buying a house together. I'm going to go out on a limb and guess there's a story there."

I sighed. *Was I ready to open up enough and talk about my very first heartbreak?* "I was madly in love with my first girlfriend. It was the first time I can honestly say another person literally took my breath away. The night she kissed me, I shook with excitement. It was the most powerful experience of my life. In many ways, I never got over that breakup. I've been guarded ever since.

"Even though it wasn't legal to get married, we had a huge ceremony. White dresses, wedding cake, invitations, the whole nine yards. We owned a house together, and I was blissfully happy. When she decided to leave me for another woman, I begged her to stay. I told her I would look the other way. She could have her affair as long as we could stay together. It was a mess untangling our finances, and I swore I would never let myself get in that position again. I haven't even considered it... until now."

Christine squeezed my hand. "Thanks for sharing that with me, and I can't tell you how honored I am you're reconsidering that ultimate commitment, as you put it. I take my commitments very seriously."

"Yeah, I believe you do. The worst part was when she threatened to take Sarasota and Freud. I nearly lost it. It was an empty threat after a particularly nasty fight. When I broke down, she realized what that would do to me, and she apologized. Ironically, it was her ex who helped me by suggesting I buy her out and that seemed to satisfy all parties. It didn't matter that I was the one who had cashed in my retirement and sold my car to come up with a down payment. I borrowed the funds to pay her off since the house had increased considerably in value from the time we'd purchased it. It was during the time of the housing market bubble, so she definitely made out like a bandit. At that point, I was just happy I got to keep my furchildren."

We continued to sit on the deck soaking in the sun and revealing bits and pieces of our life. Like the concentric circles in a tree trunk, each new ring revealed something new and underscored the vast experiences as women who'd survived many years on the planet. New relationships were far more interesting as a person aged because there was so much more to learn about the other individual. I suspected it would be many years before we knew most everything about one another. And even then, there are always those secrets a person never shares with anyone.

CHAPTER THIRTY-ONE

Colette

I didn't have any contact with Melissa for several months as I focused all my efforts on finishing school. I decided I owed it to her to see if the woman she was seeing was *the one*. I knew deep down, even though I loved Melissa, we weren't healthy for one another. I wanted someone who was a bit less reserved with their emotions. I craved an equal partner, not someone who would take care of everything for me. For too long, I'd let her do that, and now that I was standing on my own two feet, it felt good. She needed an equal partner too, someone she wouldn't have to carry the load for.

I felt proud of myself that I had a job lined up already. Actually, I had two. I was going to move back to the island and pick up part-time work at the hospital on the island, and per diem shifts at the hospital in Sedro Wooley. The night shift was a new thing to me, but I'd adjust.

My old boss at the Captain Whidbey Inn was recently divorced and offered to have me move in with him. He'd mentioned possibly working toward an arrangement where we would co-own the house. It sounded perfect.

It was time to move my dresser. I was amazed Melissa hadn't balked before now. Not only had I left her alone, but I'd also left the dresser sitting exactly in the same spot without offering to move it before now.

I picked up the phone to make the call to let her know I'd drive there this coming weekend. I knew Jo would help me move it.

After four rings, my call went to voicemail. I left a message.

"Hey, I wanted to make arrangements to pick up my dresser. I'll be moving into Stan's place. He offered to let me drop off the dresser before my official move date. Give me a call, and we can schedule a time."

Next, I needed to call Jo to see if she was free to help me out. She answered on the second ring.

"Hey, beautiful."

"Hi, Jo. I was wondering if you were free this weekend to give me a hand with my dresser."

"Wow, you're finally getting around to moving that thing. I thought you'd donated that to Melissa after all this time."

I cringed. It reminded me of how often I took advantage of Melissa's good nature. The dogs were still residing at her house on the island.

217

"No, I have a place lined up for after I complete school with my former boss, so I have a home to take it to."

"Damn, don't remind me. I know it isn't that far to the island, but I wished you'd taken a job in Seattle."

"It's too expensive to live in Seattle."

"You coulda moved in with me."

I pointedly ignored that comment. We'd become friends, and unfortunately, I'd let it drift into the friends with benefits category, but at least I'd made it clear a committed relationship was not on the table as an option.

"So, are you free to help or not?"

"Course. I'll pick you up on Saturday. What time?"

"How does ten sound?"

"Perfect. I'll pick up bagels and coffee."

"You're a peach. See ya on Saturday." She was good to me. Why couldn't I fall for the sweet ones?

The minute I ended the call with Jo, my phone rang. It was Melissa.

"Hey."

"Um, you called." She sounded nervous.

I laughed. "Relax. I know you've been more than patient with me. I wanted to make arrangements to pick up my dresser. Jo is available this weekend, so I thought it would work out well to pick it up around noon."

"Oh, well, I'll be gone this weekend. There's a weekend rainbow ride on Vashon. You have keys, just let yourself in."

"Oh yeah, that's right. Okay, if you're sure you don't mind."

"No, not at all."

"Hey, how are you doing?"

Her voice perked up. "Good, really good. I'll get to see both my sisters and my nephews at Thanksgiving. My mom is thrilled to have us all there."

"Is Christine going?" I felt a pang of jealousy. I'd loved my time visiting Melissa's parents in Florida.

"Yeah, she is."

"That's nice. Hey, I gotta go. Thanks, Melissa. Oh, and I'll get Red and Blackie out of your hair soon too. As soon as I make the move back to the island…"

"You're moving back to the island?"

"Yeah, I got a job at Whidbey. It starts a week after I finish school and become certified."

"That's great, good for you." She sounded a little wistful.

"Talk to you later."

"Okay, bye." Melissa ended the call.

†

When we arrived at Melissa's house in Cle Elum, Jo gave me an odd look as I pulled out my key and let myself in. There was a strange car in the driveway, and I assumed it was Christine's and she was on the weekend ride with Melissa.

"You have a key to your ex's house?" she asked.

I hadn't given it a lot of thought until this moment. "Uh, yeah. I guess I never gave it back to her."

"Um, I've heard of lesbians staying good friends after breaking up, but don't you think still having her key is a little…"

I ignored the critique of my continued connection to my ex because it smacked of unfounded jealousy. "It makes it easy to pick up the dresser."

"Okay, whatever."

We entered the house, and it was neat and tidy as always. The cats both greeted us at the door, and Freud began weaving his body through my legs and then through Jo's. Sarasota eyed Jo cautiously, but eventually, walked close enough for me to bend over and pet her.

"Hey, guys." I turned to Jo. "I should put these two in the bedroom while we're moving the dresser so they don't get caught underfoot and cause a catastrophe."

Jo squinted at the cats. Even though Freud was being his normal friendly self, she looked at them with mistrust. Jo was clearly a dog person.

I looked at the dresser sitting there all alone against the wall. This was the last reminder, the final tentative thread between my old life with Melissa. I was about to snip that thread. She wouldn't have the reminder of our past relationship staring her in the face every day. I wondered how she was able to ignore it, or if this was a painful thorn in her side. The sudden realization of how cruel I'd been not to remove the dresser earlier smacked me in the face. What could I possibly do to redeem myself, other than to let her have her happily ever after with Christine?

I vowed, right then and there, if there was ever anything she needed, I would move heaven and earth to make it happen. She deserved that and more from me.

"Let me clean out the litter box first, and then I'll put the cats in the bedroom."

I went in search of the litter box. The least I could do was clean that out for her. I didn't know if she'd arranged for someone to come by and do that, but I knew the cats always preferred a clean box. Sarasota followed me down the stairs, watching intently. I giggled when I had the absurd thought that maybe she was making sure I wasn't about to steal anything from her mommy.

"Stop looking at me like I'm some kind of thief."

There wasn't a lot in the box, so I presumed Melissa had employed someone to clean it out regularly while she was gone. I marched back upstairs with Sarasota following me.

You'd think I'd put the cats in a torture chamber as I heard the howling from the other side of the bedroom door. "Shhh, I'll let you out in a minute. Sheesh."

The dresser was a pain in the ass to move, but we finally managed to get it loaded into Jo's truck, and as I shut the door to Melissa's chalet, I felt a small amount of closure. I hoped when she returned from her weekend on Vashon, she would feel the same and the thorn would finally loosen and fall to the ground.

CHAPTER THIRTY-TWO

Sarasota

I jumped from the bed, and Freud followed me as soon as I heard the key in the door. I hadn't expected Melissa and Christine home so early. She'd told me they were going to be gone for the weekend, and I should be good. As if I needed someone to tell me to be good.

The last person I expected to see coming through the front door was Colette. Freud started weaving in and out of her legs and the legs of the sourpuss that had tagged along with her. I didn't like her friend at all. She looked at us with disdain. Disdain. *Can you imagine that?*

I waited a few seconds before I walked closer to Colette. I knew she wanted to pet me. Who wouldn't? *Okay, don't answer that question.* I know that poor excuse for a human being standing next to Colette wouldn't.

I was trying to figure out what Colette was doing here when she walked down the stairs. *Oh, no you don't, girlfriend. I'm not letting you steal from Melissa.* I followed her.

She knew I wasn't going to let her get away with anything. She tried to put me at ease when she said, "Stop looking at me like I'm some kind of thief," but I wasn't budging.

I was glad when she only cleaned out our litter box. I didn't relish scratching her eyes out, but I would have if she'd made one false move.

I followed her back up the stairs, and before I knew it, she had Freud and me in her arms, and unceremoniously dumped us off into the bedroom and shut the door. She'd locked us in. The nerve. Well, I wasn't going to let this transgression go without giving her a piece of my mind. I started howling, and Freud joined in. She was stealing Melissa's furniture, I could hear her. I started yowling louder.

Finally, the noises stopped, and the door opened. I rushed out, and the only thing I saw missing was the big dresser I knew didn't belong in the living room. Whew. She hadn't robbed us blind.

She looked kind of sad as she hugged and kissed us both right before she left. I let her. For some reason, I knew this would probably be the last time I ever saw Colette. I guess she needed the closure.

CHAPTER THIRTY-THREE

Melissa

We were giggling about the weekend and how much teasing the group was giving mostly me, but they included Christine in their fun.

The whole weekend we were the butt of everyone's jokes, and they teased me mercilessly.

Nadine's partner, Sammie said, "Melissa, that was the slowest pace I've ever seen you do. We knew it was love."

That wasn't the only teasing because I had also invited several other women on the weekend ride. Apparently, there was some confusion about which day they were riding, so the Rainbow Riders planned a ride for both Saturday and Sunday. The other women I invited showed up on Sunday. I could only make it on Saturday. A few new women were asking where I was. Of course, they had to embellish a little and say I left a trail of broken hearts when I chose Christine. I think they were happy to see me smile again.

Christine was teasing me about what she'd learned over the weekend about that first ride as we walked up the steps to enter the dark house. We decided to drop our bags off first before undoing the bikes.

"So, I wasn't the only woman you had dangling on a string. Just how many women did you invite to that first ride?"

I gently smacked her on the arm. "It wasn't like that. I only wanted to have people to ride with."

"Uh huh. I'm glad you told me Saturday, so I had a leg up on the competition."

"You secured your place in my heart with that first smile and the bunch of lavender."

I opened the door, and the first thing I noticed, even in the dark, was the missing dresser. I'd forgotten for a minute that Colette was going to pick it up this weekend.

Christine frowned. "Colette's dresser is gone."

"Yeah, she called on Friday and said she and a friend would be by to pick it up."

"How'd she get in?"

"She has a key."

Christine's frown deepened. "Colette has a key to your house?"

Uh oh. Her words were clipped. "Um, yeah. I never asked for it back."

"I'm not very comfortable knowing your ex can come strolling in at any time. Interrupting whatever."

"I guess I never considered that."

"Look, it's your house, your decision, but I think you should get the key back. It feels like…"

"Like I'm still too connected to my ex and haven't let go of that relationship," I finished for her.

"Well?"

"I made my decision two months ago. I guess I didn't quite know how to ask for the key back, and honestly, until Friday when I talked to her, I'd forgotten all about it."

"I'll pay for new locks."

I thought that was a little drastic, but I could tell she was pissed, and I didn't quite know what to do with that. I'd yet to see her angry.

"I don't think that's necessary. I'll ask her for the key back."

"When?"

"I don't know. The next time I talk to her."

"Do you talk to her regularly?"

This was getting out of hand. Our first fight. "No. Look, I don't want to fight about this."

"I should leave. Create some space."

"Don't be ridiculous. It's eight, you won't be home until well after ten, and then you'll have to get up at five."

"I'm angry, and a two-and-a-half-hour drive will do me a world of good. Perhaps allow me to gain perspective and not say anything I don't mean."

"Fine. You're an adult. I won't stop you." Now I was pissed.

I crossed my arms and watched as she undid her bike and repositioned it on her car. At least when she came back into the house to grab her bag, she kissed me on the lips and said, "I'll talk to you tomorrow. I love you."

"Okay." I was hurt. I let her leave without returning the sentiment. I did love her, but my pride was winning out.

†

The next day I walked into work with a scowl on my face. I entered the office and greeted Mary. I must not have said hello accompanied by a smile, as was my usual greeting.

"What's up? Did we get a grievance this morning or something?"

"No."

"Cryptic. Must be trouble in paradise. What happened? I thought you two were going to Vashon this weekend. Now I know that eight hours on a bike is not my cup of tea, but you love that stuff."

"Christine and I had a… oh, I don't know what to call it… misunderstanding, disagreement, failure to communicate. Take your pick?"

"Ah. The first fight is always the hardest. However, it sets up how you'll argue in the future. Did she stay to work it out?"

"No."

Mary cringed. "Oh, a runner."

I narrowed my eyes at her. "Well, if you're so good at interpreting relationship-speak, maybe you can help me understand why she would be so pissed."

"Hmm. I need more details."

"Well, we were coming back from Vashon. Laughing and she was teasing me about when I invited all those women to the bike ride."

227

"Jealousy? Was she teasing or was there a note of irritation in her voice?"

"No, it was definitely teasing. That isn't what set her off. We got into the house, and the dresser was gone."

Mary looked puzzled. "Why would that be a problem? I would imagine that's a good thing. Sheesh, you're far more forgiving and patient than I would have been. Wood makes an extremely cleansing bonfire."

I chuckled despite my foul mood. Mary was a Scorpio, and boy, was it not a good idea to get on her bad side. They never forgave. I was sure if she ever caught her husband cheating, he'd lose that dangling thing men are so proud of.

"The dresser being gone wasn't exactly the issue. She was irritated that Colette still has a key and let herself in to pick up her dresser while we were gone."

"Oh. That makes sense."

"What makes sense?"

"Seriously? Are you so naïve to think your ex still having a key to your place wouldn't upset Christine? What if you two were, you know, and she walked in on you? I'd be pissed too. It's bad enough you let her keep that dresser there for so long and the dogs at your place on the island. It's like you're still connected. Snip, snip, Melissa. Cut those ties and get the darned key back pronto."

I sat down heavily in the chair in her office. "She should trust me when I say it's over."

"Just because you give away your trust like beads at Mardi gras doesn't mean everyone else is wired like you. Most of us have sense enough to wait until someone has earned that trust."

"But lesbians are different. We don't stop hanging out or being friends because a relationship ends. Heck, Colette was in a band with my ex, and we all hung out together."

"Freaks. I mean that in a very non-judgmental accepting way. I could never be a lesbian then because after I cut off his thing, I don't think we'd continue to be friends."

That earned a hearty laugh from me. "So, you think she has a reason to be upset?"

"Yeah, I do. And I think you need to set your boundaries a bit better. Colette's truck has been blasting through those huge holes you've allowed. Give Christine some space today and then call tonight and apologize. Being nice is fine unless it begins to affect your new relationship and then you need to find that inner bitch." Mary shook her head. "I fear it doesn't exist in you. Maybe I should give you a little of mine. I have plenty to spare."

"Thanks, Mary."

"Anytime. That'll be a two-dollar raise please."

"Oh, you're definitely worth it. Let me see what I can do." She *was* definitely worth it. I knew if I ever lost Mary, I would have to replace her with two people.

†

I stayed late that night to finish a few projects I had going. I suppose I might have been trying to delay the inevitable phone call I knew I would make once I got home.

I was surprised to see Christine's car in my driveway. At least I was smart enough to give her a set of keys to the house.

I took a deep breath before I entered the chalet. Christine was sitting on the couch with the cats. Freud was in her lap, and Sarasota plastered herself on Christine's left side. I sat down on the other side.

"Hi, I'm glad you're here…."

"I wanted to apologize," we both said at the same time.

"Me first," I said. "My co-worker gave me a dose of reality."

She raised her eyebrow.

"Mary is very blunt. She basically said I was an idiot and too nice. The truth is I don't deal well with confrontation in my personal life. I let people walk all over me. I didn't know how to ask for the keys back without it sounding petty and mean."

"You're very trusting. That's something I admire and love about you. I don't want you to change because I have insecurities. Unfounded, I hope. Colette still has a connection to you. You still love her. I get that."

"I do still love her and want the best for her, but I'm not in love with her anymore. She killed that. If I can help her out, I will, like I would any good friend. I've always maintained friendships with my exes. Hate is a strong emotion I can't conjure up, no matter what."

"Good for you. That's admirable. I haven't stayed in contact with my exes except when necessary to make arrangements for my daughter. And if it wasn't for that connection with her that I desperately want to maintain, I'd never talk to my ex again. Staying friends is a foreign concept to me."

I held out my hand. "Give it to me?"

"What?"

"Your lesbian card. It's been revoked. Don't you know the unwritten rule to always stay friends with your exes?"

Finally, she laughed. "I would think I've earned the right to keep it with my talented fingers and tongue."

"Hmm, good point."

It wasn't the last time we would have a disagreement about Colette, but as the years came and went, Christine lost her insecurities. I would give something to Christine I never gave to Colette—a true commitment.

CHAPTER THIRTY-FOUR

Colette

I settled into my place on the island—and after I started back at Whidbey General, a sort of thawing occurred with my old friends. I suppose enough time and distance made the difference. Lanie was the first to make contact. I wasn't surprised since I'd known her the longest.

Soon after I'd retrieved my dresser, I called Melissa to see how she was doing. It was an awkward conversation, and I could tell how uncomfortable she was talking to me. I sensed something had occurred between her and Christine, but I didn't pry. She asked for the key back, and I mailed it to her.

I kept in contact, and our brief phone conversations got easier over time. Out of the blue one day, I called. It was springtime, and when I saw the deer in the back of my yard, I thought of Melissa and how she transformed into a little girl when she fed the deer apples out of her hand on Orcas Island.

I learned she was coming that weekend to take care of the house. Candie hadn't been doing a stellar job with that. Melissa had finally convinced her parents to leave Florida and move to Whidbey to take over the care of the place. I wondered why Christine wasn't coming with her but didn't ask. It had been a long time since we'd seen each other, so I suggested getting together for breakfast. She was tentative with her yes, but agreed.

We met in Coupeville at nine-thirty. It was halfway between my place and her house in Oak Harbor. She walked into the restaurant, and I stood up and waved at her. I'd already secured a booth. We shared a brief hug before she slid into the opposite side of the booth.

She looked good. I noticed she had picked up a few needed pounds and was nearly back to her original weight before we split. That told me a lot. She was happy. I was glad. At forty-five, she looked at least ten years younger. Not one single gray hair marred her beautiful hair. We shared a hairdresser who always used to say Melissa had perfect hair. She did. I was five years younger than her, and I already needed to dye my hair because the gray was taking over. She'd gone back to wearing blue contacts again, and I wondered why since after her Lasik surgery I knew she didn't need them for distance. I missed her warm brown eyes.

"You look good," I said.

She blushed. "You do too. How's night shift? Isn't it hard to make the transition from days to nights?"

I shrugged. "Why are you wearing contacts again?"

"I got tired of losing my granny glasses. Monocular vision. It helps with reading that itty-bitty print, especially since the length of my arms won't cooperate and grow a little longer so I can hold the reports at arm's length while I read."

"I liked your brown eyes."

"Yeah, but they never got noticed like my blue eyes. I don't care that they're fake. I like matching my eye color with my outfits. Some women obsess over shoes. I guess I obsess over eye color."

"So, what's this I hear about your parents moving into your house?"

"Ever since Dad retired, they've been spending like drunken sailors, and now they're worried they won't have enough money. It's a win-win. Candie doesn't take great care of the house. Did you know I had to pay her electric and gas bill? I sent colleagues to Whidbey to observe their orientation so we could create something similar at Kittitas, and they stayed at my house. Candie didn't pay the bill, and the city turned the electricity off. That's how I found out."

"You let her stay there for free?"

I shook my head. "I know, I know. Anyway, in addition to that, I had to mow grass nearly up to my waist and don't even get me started on the blackberry bushes I had to remove. That was a bowl of laughs. With my parents living here, I know they will take great care of the place. The inside will be spotless, and Dad will have a field day with the pond and taking care of any plants Christine puts in. She has an amazing green thumb."

"So, you two are still going strong, huh?"

She grinned. "Yeah, we're talking about her maybe moving into the chalet considering she spends a lot of time there already."

"Doesn't she work in Seattle?"

"Yeah, but the commute from my house isn't much different than the commute from her place. I-5 is a lot worse than I-90. Besides, she found a rideshare group, and Children's pays a portion of the costs. There's a lot of people that commute into Seattle from Cle Elum. There's even a person in her group that comes from Ellensburg."

"That's great, Melissa."

"We've been looking at houses. Something a little bigger with land."

"How are you gonna afford that?" I held up my hand. "Never mind. That's none of my business."

"It's okay. She's going to rent her house and then she would sell it if we found something we liked. I would also sell my Cle Elum house."

My eyebrow arched in response. "Wow, you must be serious if you're considering buying a house with her. I thought you'd never do that again. Once burned you weren't going to get near that fire again."

Melissa had a dopey grin. "She's the one. The one who I'm finally going to grow old with. I found what I was looking for. We fit. Oh, we fight sometimes, all couples do, but we're committed to working through anything that comes up."

I grabbed her hand and squeezed. I was genuinely happy for her. "I'm happy for you. I get the impression she doesn't care much for me. Sorry about the key causing you problems. Does she know we're meeting for breakfast?"

She nodded. "Of course. Honestly, I don't think she's jumping for joy about it, but she isn't worried anymore. I think she wonders how often we talk. In her head, it's a lot more often than it really is. During the Super Bowl, when you called, well, let's just say she wasn't thrilled about that. For such a put together, confident, woman, she has her moments of insecurity, and I'm too boneheaded to always recognize when she needs reassurance. But we always get to the other side together, and that's what counts. How about you? Are you seeing anyone?"

I shook my head. "No, and being single is what I need right now. I sort of dated Jo for a short time. You know the one who helped with the dresser, but I knew it was never a match made in heaven. Stan's been the perfect roommate, and I'm excited about all the work we're doing on the house."

"How does that work? Did he put you on the mortgage?"

"Not yet."

"You should see a lawyer and get whatever agreement you have with him in writing."

"That's new, you being the cautious one."

"I guess. I still like to assume good intentions, but it never hurts to make things clear in writing. Christine and I are going to do a kind of prenup agreement."

I was shocked by this. "Really?"

"Yeah, it was a way to get over my hang-up about buying a house together." Melissa shrugged. "Compromise. It works. I'm trusting, not stupid. I know it's not sexy or romantic, but it gives me peace of mind. Christine is very pragmatic. I love that about her. It was her suggestion."

We ate our breakfast and talked about our mutual friends. It was an easy breakfast, and in a way, it brought a level of closure to our relationship that hadn't been there before. If I'd known at the time, this would be the last time, I would ever see Melissa, I probably would have clung to her a little longer when she hugged me goodbye.

CHAPTER THIRTY-FIVE

Melissa

I was thrilled when my parents moved into my house on Whidbey in June. Even though I cleaned the house thoroughly, Mom went back over every nook and cranny again and maintained a spotless appearance every time I visited. I tried to drive up to the island at least once a month. It was nice having them so close after not living near them for so many years.

Mom found all the bingo halls and the Swinomish casino which was only a short distance away. She was quite proficient with the slot machines and always ended up ahead of the game. When I would visit, she would show me her drawer of money. The summer and fall were a delightful time for my parents, and they explored their new town. I'd set Dad up with the best internist in town. They seemed happy.

In all the time I'd lived on Whidbey, it never snowed as much as it did that winter. The temperatures were way below normal. It did not endear my mom and dad to the location, and I could see signs of strain on them both. They'd lived too long in Florida, and their thin skin could not adjust to the cold.

Mid-January, I got a call from Mom. She was anxious about Dad. He'd spent the night in the emergency department, but they weren't going to admit him for his severe episode of bronchitis. He was used to the ED physician admitting him the minute he got bronchitis when he lived in Florida and couldn't understand why they sent him home.

I tried to explain he shouldn't want to be in the hospital because it wasn't a great place to hang out unless you needed to be there. Too many people picked up hospital-acquired infections, and that made things worse. He sounded so miserable, and Mom was worried, so I called someone I knew would help out. I had connections at Whidbey, and now I knew a competent respiratory therapist.

It was Sunday morning when I made the call. I'd barely hung up the phone with Mom when I called Colette.

"Hello," Colette answered groggily.

"Damn, I thought I would catch you before you went to sleep."

"It's okay. What's wrong, Melissa? You sound a little stressed."

"Can I ask a favor?"

"Sure."

"Dad spent the better part of last night in the emergency department."

"I know. I heard."

"Why didn't you call me?"

"HIPAA. You remember that little law. It has quite the bite when you violate it."

"Sorry, sorry. You're right. Anyway, do you think you can go to the house and check Dad out? Make sure he doesn't need to be in the hospital or doesn't have pneumonia like he seems to think."

"Sure, I'll grab a pulse oximeter and see what his oxygen levels are."

I breathed a sigh of relief. "Thanks. I owe you."

"No, you don't. I love your parents. They were always good to me. Um… You better call your mom and warn her I'm coming over."

"I will. It's been enough time. I'm sure she's over, um, her rant."

"I hope so." Colette chuckled.

"Will you call me after you see him and give me a report?"

"Of course. Hey, don't worry. I'm sure he's miserable but not in any real danger."

"Thanks, Colette."

"Anytime."

I ended the call and was grateful Colette would be there for my father. I knew she would make a great therapist. Even though we'd ended things over a year ago, Colette was a kind and compassionate human being and a great caregiver. I got to see that firsthand when she traveled back and forth to care for her mother when she was dying.

†

Christine rolled over and reached for me. "We should get dressed and head to Whidbey."

"Sorry, hon, I didn't mean to wake you. I should have got up and made the call, or at least left the room when I phoned Mom."

She grinned. "I'm glad you didn't. It's rare I get to listen firsthand to a phone conversation between you and your ex."

I smacked her playfully. "It's not like we talk to each other every night. It's more like once every couple of months."

"I'm teasing. I know I have nothing to worry about. I'm so glad she was such a fool to let you go. Damn, you're looking awfully sexy with your messy hair."

I attempted to smooth down my unruly locks. "Hey, I worked on this 'do all night long."

"Didn't I just say how sexy you looked?"

"Join me in the shower?"

"Best offer I've had all day."

"Our day just started."

"Yeah, so, it's still the best offer."

"Coffee, please." I batted my eyes.

"I thought you wanted me in the shower?"

"I do… after you make us some coffee."

She stroked my face and blessed me with a sweet kiss. "Okay. I love you."

"I love you too."

I walked my naked body into the shower and waited for Christine to join me.

†

We were on the road in less than an hour. I wasn't sure if Colette would still be there when we arrived, but I got my answer as we hit the back roads through the tulips on the way to Highway 20.

Christine was driving, so when my cell phone rang, I answered without guilt. "Hello."

"Hey, Melissa. I just left your house. Your dad is grumpy and miserable, but he'll live. His oxygen level is not that bad. I gave him a breathing treatment, and I'll come back again tomorrow to give him another. I have to work tonight, so I better head back home to get some shut eye."

"God, you're an angel. I appreciate what you're doing. Thanks, Colette."

She chuckled. "I think the ice is melting on the iceberg."

"Huh?"

"Your mom. She hugged me before I left. Her gratitude was very genuine."

"I'm sure she was grateful for your time. She loves my dad. Goodness knows I have no idea why, but they've been married for nearly fifty years, so they must have something going that beats the odds."

"Yeah, I wish I could find that." She sounded wistful, and I was sorry she hadn't found someone like Christine to make her whole again.

"You will. Have faith. I didn't find my one and only until I was forty-five. You have a few years yet. Keep looking and be open to it when it comes your way."

After I ended the call, Christine piped up, "And I didn't find my true love until I was fifty-one. It's never too late."

"Aw, that is so sweet... I think I better see a dentist."

242

"I meant every word." She faked a huff.

"I know you did, honey. Love you."

"I'm glad Colette was there to help your dad."

"You are?"

"Yeah, I know I judge her harshly, but she must have had some redeeming qualities, or you wouldn't have spent eight years with her."

"She did."

I changed the subject after that because I didn't want to make Christine feel inadequate or let her believe I missed anything about my relationship with Colette. I thought it was natural for me to feel nostalgic on occasion, and I suspect Christine understood.

When we arrived at my parents, I realized they were getting old, and my mother was definitely mellowing with age. She praised Colette's generous care and proved she wouldn't hold a grudge until hell froze over, after all. I think she knew if I called her to help, I'd made my peace with Colette. She didn't need to be the one to come to my rescue. I was glad. I know it meant a lot to Colette, and she certainly deserved to be back in my mother's good graces. She would be losing a lot of sleep over the next few days traveling to Oak Harbor to give my father free treatments.

I felt like we were all finally at a place where we could forgive one another and accept both the good and the bad.

CHAPTER THIRTY-SIX

Colette

The years stretched out after I took care of Melissa's dad. I would call her out of the blue, or sometimes, she would call me. I never met Christine in the flesh, but I got to know her through Melissa and our other friends. I felt satisfied she was good for Melissa. I hadn't yet found my other half.

Stan had decided to sell the house we were supposed to own together. I had moved to California since I was homeless and needed a change. I hadn't made time to have a lawyer draw up a legal agreement as Melissa had suggested, so I'd lost out on a lot of money from the sale of the house.

I called her up one day after the sale. I was excited because I had met a wonderful woman and was on the verge of moving to Lake Havasu in Arizona. I knew Melissa had lived in Arizona for a couple of years after she got out of college. I wanted to catch up with her life.

"Hey, stranger," she answered. "How the heck are you? Tori said you moved to California."

I laughed. The gossip chain was alive and well. "I did for a minute, and then I met someone. Now I'm ready for a new adventure in Arizona."

"Wow, really?"

"Yeah, she's wonderful. She has two kids. I hate that she'll be paying most of the bills until I can get a full-time job. The market in Arizona is especially tight for respiratory therapists. I can probably pick up per diem work. How about you? How's it going with Christine?"

"It's great. We have our house in the country now. Three acres. Christine is in heaven. She won't let me mow the lawn because I don't get the lines correct." She laughed. "We registered as domestic partners a few years ago. We're waiting for it to be legal to marry. I can't believe I'm considering getting married again, but I think this one will finally stick."

"I'm so happy for you, Melissa."

"It's funny you called. I was listening to your CD the other day. You should record another one."

"Nah, I just play for fun now."

"What about that book you were writing about your mom? How is that coming?"

"I haven't written any more on that."

"You should go back to that. What I read was good. I hope you get full-time work soon. Hey, listen, I'm driving now, and I probably shouldn't have even taken the call, but I saw it was you..."

"No, that's okay. Catching up a little bit was good. I'll talk to you later."

"Yeah, bye, Colette."

I settled back in my chair and looked around at all my boxes. I had accumulated a lot since my move back to the island. We'd rented a U-Haul, and I was waiting for my new lover to return before tossing all my belongings into the back and heading to Lake Havasu. I chuckled at the old joke about U-Hauls because that certainly fit this situation. I'd met her a month ago when she was in Seattle for a conference. She was a nurse, and we'd hit it off right away. Maybe I was destined for my happily ever after like Melissa.

†

Six months later, Melissa called. She said she was thinking about me and wanted to know how I was doing. She sounded concerned. I didn't know how she knew, some kind of spidey sense I suppose, but I was getting ready to move back to California.

"Hey," I answered.

"I was thinking about you and wanted to call and see how you were doing?"

"Did the grapevine tell you?"

"No, what's up."

"I'm moving to California."

"Oh… I'm sorry. I guess that means things didn't work out."

"No, the financial pressures were too great on her. I never could find full-time work. On the bright side, I got a full-time job in California. That's why I'm moving there. Plus, I get to live by my sister, Isabella. I start next week."

"That's great. Maybe California is where you're meant to be."

"I'm hoping this will be the last time I move. How are things going with you?"

"They're great, although the CEO I work with is leaving, and that's always unsettling. I've loved working with him. We'll see what happens. I have a great team, so that's half the battle."

We continued to talk for a few more minutes. All small talk. It was clear our lives had taken two very distinctive paths away from each other. Our contact continued to be farther and farther apart as the years progressed.

CHAPTER THIRTY-SEVEN

Sarasota

I know I scared Melissa today when I had my seizure, and Freud kept hovering around me all worried that I would keel over any minute. I was old, and I was tired. It was time. I wanted Melissa to let me go, but she wouldn't. She took me to the vet, a place I despise, and kept giving me this medication at the first sign of the next seizure.

Today was a bad one, and I'd lost the use of my back legs. I kept purring for her because I knew that's what she wanted. When Christine came home from work and hugged Melissa, telling her everything would be all right, I knew she was in good hands. She wouldn't need me anymore. Freud was an old man, so I knew I'd see him soon. I wanted Melissa to get a new kitten because, frankly, we enriched a human's life.

"Baby, it's time," Christine said.

"I don't know if I can do it." Melissa started crying again.

"There's a vet who will come to the house. You can hold Sarasota until the end."

Oh, thank God. I hoped Melissa was going to listen.

"Meow." It wasn't a strong response, but I hoped she understood my addition to the conversation. I told her it was okay. It was what I wanted. What I needed. My time had come.

"You make the call please, I can't do it."

"I will."

A very kind woman came to the house, and while I laid in Melissa's arms, she gave me my last shot on earth. I passed away peacefully. Freud joined me one month later, and we watch over Melissa.

I was glad when she decided to never get another Himalayan because there were too many cats and kittens that needed homes and rescuing. Besides, she'd said we could never be replaced. That was the right answer.

Several years later, when she gave Ebony a home, I was proud that she'd taken a chance on another black cat. He was trouble with a capital T at first, but he kept her company during those long nights when she and Christine were apart. I knew they'd make it, though, because they had that kind of love.

CHAPTER THIRTY-EIGHT

Melissa

Christine and I had just attended one of those mandatory fun events we both hate going to, but since it's an expectation for all the senior leaders, she's a good sport about it. After we returned home, she noted the new CFO was probably a bit homophobic. She sat at our table. Christine was always more observant about these things than I ever was.

"Didn't you see how she reacted when Karl went on stage, and the guy was teasing him?" she asked.

Karl was our CNO, and he was an out gay man who always brought his partner to these events, just like me. I never gave it a second thought because when I had interviewed for the job eight years prior, I made it clear that if me being a lesbian was going to be an issue, I wasn't interested. The recruiter assured me it was not a problem because the CNO was openly gay.

"I don't have a handle on her yet. I'm not very impressed, and I was surprised when the CEO let Harry go, but I have to trust he knows what he's doing."

"I have a bad feeling," Christine said.

†

The next day, the CEO called the management team to the second-floor conference room for an emergency meeting. I sat in shock as he relayed his plan for restructure and the promotion of the quality director to the CNO position because Karl was no longer with our hospital.

Christine was right. There was something terribly rotten happening at the hospital I had loved working at for so many years. The restructure meant human resources would no longer have a seat at the C-suite table. I still had all the departments under me that I'd previously supervised, but I would no longer be a part of the senior leadership team.

I had a lot to discuss with Christine when I came home that evening. Her commute into Seattle normally meant she wouldn't arrive until late, so my news would have to wait.

I was in bed reading when she walked up the stairs. My eyes met hers, and she asked, "What's wrong?"

"They fired Karl today and restructured the management team."

"What?"

"You heard me. I think you're right about the CFO. I hate to say this, but I'm worried. I'm the last of the senior leaders leftover from our original team. If it wasn't for the

251

fact that they need me to negotiate the contracts, I'm pretty sure I'd be gone too."

Christine sat heavily on the bed. "Okay. We'll get through this."

My eyes teared up. "So much for our plans to retire here."

"Let's not get ahead of ourselves. Something will come up. You're very well respected. Aren't you getting that big award in September?"

"Yeah."

"Any organization would be lucky to have you."

"I've already started looking. There's an opening at Samaritan in Moses Lake. The cost of living there is very cheap. I think we could make that work and still stay on track to retire when I'm sixty. Sorry, babe, but if we want to keep the house, you'll need to continue to work."

"I know."

I had my laptop open to a real estate page where a condo on the lake looked very inviting. "Hey, come here and take a look at this."

She crawled next to me on the bed and peered over my shoulder. "Looks nice."

"If I get the job, we should buy a condo. Then we would have a lakeside vacation place to go to after retirement."

"Hmm. I do like the water. Oh, look. There's a pool in the complex. Even better."

†

Four months later, I started at Samaritan in Moses Lake, and we bought that condo on the lake. Living apart for four years was a testament to the strength of our relationship.

Three months after I started at my new job, same-sex marriage became legal in the state. Neither of us planned a big romantic gesture, getting down on one knee to ask the other. We simply started talking about what we'd like to plan for a wedding.

By the springtime, we'd set a date. I asked my older sister when it was best for her, and we planned the event around her school schedule. She had a break in August, and that worked out perfectly for us because we wanted to have an outdoor wedding in our backyard.

Our wedding was non-traditional, to say the least. Christine wanted to have elements of the Buddhist faith in the ceremony, and I didn't care about the ceremony itself. We planned a very small affair with only our closest friends and family. Our favorite sushi restaurant agreed to cater the event, and we received rave reviews from everyone who was able to make it.

We incorporated two of our nephews into the ceremony. A good friend who was an engineer at my former hospital was our officiate. After many hours of listening to music, we finally decided on Brandi Carlisle's "The Story" as the song we would use as we walked together up the path to the stone bench under what I lovingly referred to as our granny tree. By this time in our life, we both had numerous lines across our face, mirroring the lyrics to the song. Those lines and those life experiences brought us to this place in our lives. While nothing is perfect, perfection is overrated. Growth is far more satisfying.

The only parent left alive to witness our joining was my father. I'd lost my mother the year before, and one short month before our ceremony, Christine's mother had died. We played two songs in their honor and took a moment of reflection, hoping that somehow, they were cheering us on from the great beyond. I glanced at my father when "Only Time" by Enya came on, which was my mother's favorite song, and saw the tears in his eyes. He was still struggling with that loss.

I wanted to believe my mother was watching over me, and yet it kind of freaked me out to consider that. I knew I had a warped train of thought when I pondered if she could see us when we were, you know, in the throes of passion, or when I was taking care of myself because Christine and I lived apart during the week.

I was glad when Christine offered to take the lead with the words and vows at our ceremony. I hadn't the foggiest idea what I would say.

One weekend before the ceremony, when we were both at the house in Cle Elum, she read to me what she wrote. "Nothing happens without cause. An old oriental saying reveals that even the brushing of one's sleeve against a stranger's sleeve on a ferry may be the cause of their future encounters. The union of Christine and Melissa is not accidental. The law of Karma, the inexorable unfolding of the truth of interdependence, it is an inevitable consequence of all actions. They, from the very beginning, have been coming together toward this sacred moment. Therefore, this union must never be broken or dissolved." I loved that she wrote this for us.

"That's perfect. Even though you know I'm not spiritual. One concept I have embraced is Karma," I responded. At that moment, I believed that all the time I had lived an honest life and tried as best I could to be kind to others was finally paying off.

The next two-and-a-half years of our marriage would test our resolve to remain together. It wasn't easy commuting on the weekends. We were both very lonely in the evenings, but we made it work.

I got lonely at night, and when a co-worker posted a picture of a fluffy black kitten, I answered the ad and adopted him. Since he was all black, we called him Ebony. He was an affectionate little tike and cuddled with me like Sarasota had always done. Sometimes, I thought maybe Sarasota had sent him to me knowing I needed a little furball at the condo.

On a lark, I decided to start writing. I had a lot of extra time on my hands in the evenings, and I didn't want to waste it away watching television. Most of the time, I would read, and one night, I thought to myself, I could write lesbian fiction, so in a few short months, I had my first manuscript ready to send out.

Affinity e-book press sent an e-mail stating they wanted to set up a Skype call to talk about my manuscript. I was so nervous talking to authors I had read and admired. It was like speaking to royalty. They didn't pull any punches. They thought my story had potential, but it needed a lot of help. I'd made a lot of rookie mistakes. One of the owners agreed to work with me to see if they could whip the manuscript into shape enough to make it publishable. We spent the next three months doing exactly that.

I worked hard, and in the spring of the following year after our marriage, I had a published novel. It didn't sell well, but that didn't stop me from writing another book that ended up selling well enough to get my name out there. I was developing a following. Christine was proud of me, and writing gobbled up my free time, but I still felt lonely in the evenings without my wife by my side.

Finally, we tired of living apart and made the decision to sell the house we loved so much. I felt more settled about the sale than Christine, but she agreed that if we were to meet our timeline for retirement, and she could leave a job she hated, the house had to go.

Karma is an interesting beast. Hours after we agreed to the price a buyer had offered, Christine got a call. The perfect position had opened, and they wanted her. She could work from home. She came out of her single day of retirement, and we started making plans to scale down our belongings so everything would fit in the condo.

This was the ultimate test of our relationship. I had items I simply could not part with, and so did she. Compromise is not always easy, but eventually, we got there.

†

Christine and I have been together now for nearly fifteen years and married for almost six. I never thought I would get married again. Don't forget, I'd been burned before by artist number one, number two, and number three, but I'm sure that this time it will work. Christine is already my longest relationship, and she's not an artist, so I think I'm safe now.

256

I called Colette two years ago and asked her if she would co-author our story. In our phone conversation, she updated me on her life. Shortly after she moved to California and began her job, she became ill. Her kidneys were failing, and she had started dialysis. She'd met another woman, and they are still going strong after five years. Colette's been on a list for a new kidney, and I haven't spoken with her since, so I don't know if she ever received one. She had mentioned she was on the verge of finally receiving disability and that would help her contribute to the family finances with her new lover.

I sent her the beginnings of the manuscript. I wanted to be fair and represent her perspective without judgment. Initially, she said she would, but after reading what I had written, she decided it was too painful. I thought that was a shame because Colette is a brilliant writer and she would have made this story great. She asked me not to write the story, and so I put it on a shelf.

A few weeks ago, I experienced my own life-changing event and decided to dust off the beginnings of my love story. For the first time, I'm writing a simple love story, no special effects or mash-ups like I'm known for. I decided our story needed telling. I've played fast and loose with a few details, and have imagined Colette's perspective, so this is definitely fiction. I've changed the names to protect the innocent—or guilty depending on your perspective. I wanted the world to see what a wonderful woman my wife is and how she completes me. Her support of my early retirement is unwavering, even though I am still struggling with it, but that's a whole new story that perhaps I will pen someday.

I know I should call Colette and warn her a book might come out that I've loosely based on our lives. I want her to know I had to embellish quite a bit when writing in her voice, but I hoped what I did envision would accurately represent her point of view. I'll do that, but not until I have a contract in my hands because I'm not looking forward to that conversation. I'm sure she will feel betrayed, but that is not my intention.

It's funny now that I have fourteen published novels with another one coming out in a few months, will I be able to say I'm still in an artist-free zone? After all, aren't all writers, artists?

EPILOGUE

Ebony

Ebony jumped up on the couch when his human came home early. She grabbed her laptop like usual, but something wasn't right, so he placed a comforting paw on her lap. Something wet hit his fur. He looked up at Melissa and then licked her hand when she started to pet him.

"Meow," he asked. He was wondering what was going on. Everything seemed to be so great lately with his other mom finally living in the same place. He didn't much appreciate all of his brothers and sister living in the tiny condo, but they'd adjusted after a few weeks, and each had established their own territory.

"I was fired today, Ebony," she stated through her tears.

Ebony continued to lick her hand. He wasn't going anywhere. She needed him.

Melissa picked up her phone when it began to ring.

"Hello… They offered six months' severance… No, I'm not going to fight it. In some ways, it is a big relief…" She chuckled. "I love you too. Now you'll be the primary breadwinner until I pick up an interim assignment. Sure… An apple cider might just be the medicine I need tonight, that and your loving presence. Yes, I know. The universe will provide. It gave me you, and that's all that matters."

Ebony had never seen his human cry before. He'd seen Christine cry, but not Melissa. He was only a cat, but he knew that somehow his presence would help.

"I guess I could always become a full-time writer. If only I could make a decent living at it. I guess it's time to finish that pure romance—without the extra quirks. I better call Colette to let her know I can't honor her wishes not to write the story. I do hope she will understand." She chuckled and added, "I'm becoming what I decided to avoid in relationships, an artist. Now that's ironic. I hope you like being married to a flaky artist. How about I call the book *Artist-Free Zone*?" She laughed again.

Melissa smiled when she ended her phone call, and Ebony knew she'd be okay, especially since he was going to lay on top of her, lick her chin, and give her all the affection she needed.

ABOUT THE AUTHOR

Annette is an award-winning author, published by Affinity Rainbow Publications, who lives in the beautiful Pacific Northwest with her wife and their five furry kids. With twenty-four published novels, three Lesfic Bard Awards, and one Goldie Award for her fourth novel, *Locked Inside*, she finally feels like a real author. Annette is as much a reader as a writer and is always looking for the next lesfic novel to queue up. She came up with the One Fan at a Time tagline, because it rolled off the tongue much better than One Reader at a Time. After pondering who she was at her core, she feels it was all about connecting to each reader on a personal level. Annette would be the first to admit she doesn't do well with the masses. If someone picks up her book and it touches them, she believes she has achieved what she wants with her writing by reaching each reader. It is who she is at her core. Drop her a line, she loves to hear from readers.

Email: annettemori0859@gmail.com.

Sign up for her mailing list: http://eepurl.com/cS7nr9

Check out her blog: Everyday Occurrences:

https://annettemori0859.wordpress.com/

Visit the Affinity Rainbow Publications website for her books and many other outstanding authors:

www.affinityrainbowpublications.com

261

OTHER AFFINITY BOOKS

<u>Finding her Heart</u> by Samantha Hicks
Ellis Davis's self-imposed isolation is blown apart when a new neighbour moves in next door. Having spent the last five years working from home, shutting herself away from the world she once knew. The last thing Ellis wants, or needs, is the woman next door challenging her beliefs about herself and bringing out feelings Ellis has never experienced before.

Melissa Cole moves into her new home as a recently divorced woman, raising her young son as a single parent with the help of her parents. Melissa is instantly intrigued by her mysterious neighbour next door.

<u>Forever Home</u> by Ali Spooner
Nat, Marissa and Maggie survived their first winter by the ocean. Spring brings new growth, friends, and unwelcome visitors to the homestead. Find out how Nat and Marissa's tiny community deal with the hazards and rewards before them, as their homestead continues to grow and prosper. Expect romance, adventure, danger, good fortune, and the odd meal or two, in this sequel to The Bee Charmer.

Disconnected by Annette Mori

Vanna has always felt like something was off with her parents, leaving her feeling oddly disconnected. She decides to move across the country and establish a new and independent life after college. On the way to her new position in Flagstaff, Arizona, Vanna meets out and proud Trey, who loves to flirt.

Trey has never forgotten the beautiful young woman she met briefly and is determined to ensure their paths cross again.

Thousands of miles from home, Vanna finds out more about herself, but not her feeling of being disconnected from her parents. Will Vanna ever form the connection she desperately seeks? Does Trey's determination work out?

Darcy Comes Home by Jen Silver

After twenty-five years Darcy and Angie meet again and from the faintly flickering embers of their forbidden teenage love, a flame erupts. Family complications arise including a reluctant engagement, secret surrogacy, and a persistent ex-wife.

Villagers in Professor Darcy Belsfield's childhood home of Sycamore Haven remember her being sent away to a Christian conversion camp in Canada when her father discovered her making love to her school friend, Angie.

Angie has never married but she does have a past and some unenthusiastic plans for the future. Will the differences in their lives doom the chance of Darcy and Angie discovering if they can build a future together?

Hat Trick by Ali Spooner and K.L. Gallagher

Alexandra "Alex" Hawthorne is on the fast track to the top of one of the most formidable, white-collar, criminal defense law firms in New York. She can ill afford any distractions, especially those with dark-brown eyes, who can rock a power suit while coaching professional hockey players. Not now. Not when Alex is so close to making senior partner. Not after all she has sacrificed.

After a devastating end to her playing career, Janelle Leblanc channeled her passion into coaching and reached the pinnacle of success as the first female head coach in NHL history. Despite her accomplishments, she hears whispers that she was hired as nothing more than a publicity stunt. Janelle's focus needs to remain on the ice if she is to prove them wrong, not on a certain curly haired attorney with the most arresting emerald-green eyes she has ever seen.

Once the spark is lit, their chemistry is impossible to ignore. Can Janelle break down Alex's walls to give them a real chance? Or will Alex's past heartache be too much for them to overcome?

The Lone Star Collection *II* by Various Authors

Saddle up for a wild ride! *The Lone Star Collection II* has something for everyone! If you enjoy romance, Kris Bryant and Dena Blake have penned hot contemporary stories in *Heat* and *Horseplay*, while *Pins and Needles*, by Julie Cannon, is a historical adventure. Annette Mori also contributes to the romance fare with a beautiful, enduring love story in *Rainstorm*. If you want sizzling erotica check out *50 by 50*, from Renee Mackenzie. What would a collection be without fantasy, paranormal and swashbuckling adventures? *Lured to the Rocks*, a unique work of fantasy by Barbara Ann Wright. In *The Devil's Backbone*, Lacey L. Schmidt spins a thriller about overcoming evil and personal loss. MJ Williamz explores dark passion in *Take Me All the Way*. Del Robertson offers *Return to Me* a classic pirate story, and Yvette Murray tosses in the *Ghostly Galleons*.

Footprints by Ali Spooner
Sandy, the youngest sibling of Gator Girlz, Inc., has worshipped her older sister Cam all her life and wanted nothing more than to be just like her hero. *Footprints* provides readers with Sandy's story of growing up in the Bayous of Louisiana. When the devastating floods of 2016 impact the Baton Rouge area, Cam and Sandy join the Cajun Navy to help rescue families trapped in the rampant floodwaters. The story also revisits Sandy's victory over Bubba Gump and how Sandy's injuries started her down the path to find the love of her life. Food, adventures, and great family relationships fill the pages of *Footprints*.

Love at Leighton Lake by Samantha Hicks
Tallulah 'Tally' Roberts decides that a few weeks staying in a cabin at Leighton Lake will help mend her shattered

pelvis and broken heart.

Caitlyn Matthews works at the lake resort her mother owns, loving nothing better than spending her morning swimming in the lake. That is until she meets Tally. Their attraction is instant, but both are wary of these new feelings with their history of previous relationships.

As they get to know each other, secrets from Caitlyn's past come to light. Caitlyn fears her mother has been lying to her and together they search for the truth.

Love at Leighton Lake is packed full of love, drama, and a cow called Houdini who likes to roam the cabins, much to Caitlyn's delight.

The Others by Annette Mori

As a seer and brilliant scientist, Em convinces her wife, Lise, to prepare for the inevitable conclusion, after the chaos caused by foreign countries attacking the United States. Leaving behind a wake of destruction and a new world order, forcing them to navigate a frightening reality. After ten months in their cozy bomb shelter, they emerge to a world where the vegetation is surprisingly unaffected. Should they band together with other survivors, or try to make it on their own? There are others in this unknown world. On the first day outside of their shelter, they meet members of an alternate society. Are they friend or foe? Change is inevitable. But will they change in ways Em and Lise can live with, or will this altered world change them into something unrecognizable?

Three Mile Cache by Jen Silver
The story is set in Australia circa 1988. When archaeologist Carolyn Wells returns home to Sydney after several months away at a dig in Tunisia, she expects to be reunited with her lover, Detective Inspector Alex Graham. But she soon learns that Alex has been wounded in a hostage incident and is recuperating at a Royal Flying Doctor Service hospital at a place in the outback of New South Wales called Three Mile Cache. Carolyn decides to fly out there and surprise Alex with her arrival. Surprises abound when she gets there. One of the doctors treating Alex has a rather intimate interpretation of a bedside manner. There are mysterious goings-on at a local homestead and Alex's injuries haven't stopped her from probing into the lives of the locals, much to their annoyance. When Carolyn and Alex meet again, things don't quite work out as either of them would like. Can their relationship recover from the series of events in Three Mile Cache that threaten to keep them apart?

The Black Knight and the Lady by JM Dragon
A lady faces the bleak loss of someone who had caught her heart but never known her love at the final battle where King Arthur Pendragon is returned to the Ladies of the Lake. A knight armored in black, in search of redemption, has a personal secret that at any time could ruin the reputation of the family name.

When the lady's father, a nobleman affiliated with King Arthur, asks the Black Knight to bring his daughter home from Camelot, the knight reluctantly agrees. Neither the lady nor the Black Knight could have expected what was to follow in this timeless romance of love battling secrets and treachery.

Sculpting Her Heart by Annette Mori
On the surface, it appears as if Zari Woods has achieved everything, she set out to accomplish fame, money, a supportive best friend, and loving parents. But to a person on the neurodiverse spectrum, a loving woman is elusive. When the right woman comes along she's already taken.

Soul on Fire by Ali Spooner
A perfect summer ends with danger on the Appalachian Trail for Whit, Mitch and Brad. Once safely home, the relationship between Eli and Whit continues to strengthen as the boys return home and they grow as a couple. Eli falls deeper in love with Whit and North Carolina as the trees come alive with autumn color. The first Christmas at Cast Iron Farm is celebrated with Eli's family as a new chapter in all of their lives begins. Join the family for the third book in the Cast Iron Farm Series.

The Boss's Daughter by Samantha Hicks
Vivian Westfall, CFO of *Bridger Holdings*, meets her

boss's estranged daughter, Lauren, when a disturbance at the company spring party piques her interest. Lauren is clearly drunk and making a fool of herself. To prevent embarrassment, Vivian forces Lauren away from the party. They have angry words, and things take an unexpected turn when Lauren kisses her. Months later Lauren pitches a proposal to her father to loan her the funds to start her own health club. Her father reluctantly agrees with a caveat; Vivian must go with her to Scotland to keep an eye on the money. It doesn't take long for the sparks to fly in all emotional directions. When Gregory Bridger finds out about their relationship, he does everything in his power to break them apart. Trust is at the heart of this love story, a fragile emotion that without it, things can and do fall apart.

Affinity
Rainbow Publications

eBooks, Print, Free eBooks

Visit our website for more publications available online.

www.affinityrainbowpublications.com

Published by Affinity Rainbow Publications
A Division of Affinity eBook Press NZ LTD
Canterbury, New Zealand

Registered Company 2517228

www.ingramcontent.com/pod-product-compliance
Lightning Source LLC
Chambersburg PA
CBHW070320260626
47160CB00003B/898